Dividing Lines

The Asian Writer Short Story Prize

*Short stories on the theme of Borders,
Boundaries and Belonging*

July 2018

Dear Rosie,
I hope that
you enjoy reading.
And hope to see
you soon.
Love Meena xxx

First published 2017 by Dahlia Publishing Ltd
6 Samphire Close Hamilton
Leicester LE5 1RW
ISBN

Printed and bound by Grosvenor Group

A CIP catalogue record for this book is
available from The British Library

CONTENTS

Foreword
C. G. MENON

This anthology brings together the best of the entries for the 2016 The Asian Writer Short Story Prize – and what a wonderful selection it is! One of the significant contributions of The Asian Writer as an initiative is that it brings a wide variety of pan-Asian voices into the mainstream. It acts as a counter-example to the prevailing tendency to regard Asia – and Asian writers – as monolithic, able to represent only a single unified cultural experience.

As we might expect from the prize-winning anthology, *Dividing Lines* presents as many differing viewpoints as it does stories. Each piece is informed by a different lived Asian experience, without ever being constrained by stereotype. The settings range from Uganda to India to Scotland and span over eighty years. The protagonists are young, old, rich, poor, modern, old-fashioned and everything in between.

The theme set this year for entries was borders, boundaries and belonging. On reading this collection, I was struck by the inventive ways in which the different writers have interpreted this theme. The underlying focus – that of division – comes through clearly in the polish and technique of these pieces, despite their disparate subjects.

Many of these stories centre on people divided by war and conflict. In the gripping "Ninety Days", Ashok Patel immerses us in the terrifying experiences of an Asian family

i

forced to leave Uganda. Mona Dash's "The Boatboy" brings revolt and rebellion to life, with a stirring description of the bravery of India's youngest martyr. Meanwhile, Lynne E. Blackwood's "Cows and Lambs" draws a parallel between the role of an officer and that of a farmer, with a wonderful look at a villager and his son. All of these stories take a single moment and magnify it to show the reader a wider environment of conflict, without ever losing their compelling focus.

Several other stories in this collection examine the lines that divide us from family and friends. In these pieces the tension is internal, and the writers all skilfully take the reader into the minds of their protagonists. Farhana Khalique evokes both happiness and loss in "Under the Same Sky", a poignant examination of friendship left behind. Farrah Yusuf shows us the world of a broken family in "Mind the Gap", with a lyrical characterisation of anger and pain. Serena Patel carries us forward into a brilliantly-imagined future in "The Other Side of the Bridge", with two lovers forced apart by political change.

Belonging – or failing to belong – is another theme handled very well in this anthology. Sadia Iqbal's "The Picnic" presents a chilling tale of racism and its effects on a family. Meanwhile, Namita Elizabeth Chakrabarty uses two contrasting parties to take us into the head of a solitary woman in "Eurovision". Palo Stickland also examines the internal in "The Man in the Shadows", a supernatural tale of a woman discovering her family and a shocking secret. The protagonist in Jamilah Ahmed's delicate "The Swim" is also searching for a place to belong and a way to move on from her childhood. These writers examine what it means to be "other", creating heart-breaking moments of realism in their narratives.

Finally, a number of these stories illustrate the struggle of characters facing division from their true selves by external circumstances. Making an individual experience universal is one of the hardest challenges of writing, and these authors have excelled at it. Juhi the Fragrant presents the funny and touching "Red and Purple" where a sari is a route to personal freedom, while Meera Betab explores repression and truth with "Saviour", an intense story centred on gay sex and love in modern India. Farah Ahamed also expands on this theme in the gripping "A Safe Place", taking us through the agony of personal betrayal.

These writers have all made the theme of borders, boundaries and belonging their own, providing us with a huge variety of experiences, literary styles and subjects. *Dividing Lines* is a collection worthy of a place on any bookshelf, and an effective showcase for modern Asian writing.

Saviour
MEERA BETAB

Every wall of my father's shop was lined with shelves. Each of these were crammed high with grinders that pound down spices, hand mixers which made the smoothest of masalas and industrial sized vats that churned out enough lassi for the largest of families. My father made a good living through the shop that was well placed on the Patparganj Road. He had a number of obscure business interests and this, when combined with the shop takings was sufficient to send me, his only son to a good private school. The money also enabled my father to purchase a plot in an affluent neighbourhood in North Delhi, on which every few years a new storey to a property was added. In time, the residence stood at three storeys, far too large a home for a family of three. But I grew up knowing that those floors were intended for future generations, the children I would be obliged to bring into the world. By the time I left home at the age of twenty, the plumbing to the second and third floors had still not been connected so that the taps ran a dirty sludge and a mist of dust permeated every corner of those rooms.

On the back wall of the shop was a picture of my father shaking hands with L.K. Advani. There was a barely legible scribble of Hindi which my father would proudly read out whenever he could, 'To Shri Bhavesh Bedi, with thanks for your ceaseless campaigning work for the Bharatiya Janata Party'. I had never seen my father smile more broadly than in that picture. An ardent supporter of the leader of the BJP, my father attended monthly meetings without fail while enthusiastically campaigning for whoever the local candidate was at the time. When customers came into the shop to enquire as to the best model of blender, he would extol the virtues of the local candidate. When they came in to repair a rusty old machine beyond hope, he would not only suggest the most expensive replacement but also thrust a BJP leaflet in their hand.

As soon as I had finished my homework, my father would set me up on a stool outside the shop with a pile of leaflets with instructions to deliver them into the hands of passers-by. When I was older, he paid me a small allowance to venture into the local streets and market to distribute many more. I would eagerly take the rupees; it was enough to buy a Stardust magazine and a pack of Lucky Strikes. And then I would take the leaflets in my satchel and when I thought nobody was looking, discard them on a rubbish heap, taking care to re-arrange some of the waste on top. I had no interest in politics and would not have cared any more if the leaflets had been for the Congress Party or the Communists or for anyone else for that matter. My aim was only to find a quiet spot to sit and lust after a favourite actor while leafing through a magazine and chain-smoking as many cigarettes as possible. Then I would return to the shop and my father's muttered approval when he saw the empty bag, 'Well done Ashok, well done beta.' This was all before my parents learnt of my true nature, that I would never marry and give them the grandchildren that would fill those empty rooms.

Ten years later, I'm sitting with Mathew and Sadeeq on a bench outside the Volga restaurant in Connaught Place. With its inner and outer circles, the eight roads that truncate the middle and the twelve roads that reach out from the outer ring into the rest of Delhi, Connaught Place resembles a giant wheel. Nearby, there's another wheel; the Ashoka Chakra which sits at the centre of the tricoloured National Flag of India. Like an automatic reflex, the words of the second President of India which I have learnt by rote as a child come to me, 'The wheel denotes motion. There is death in stagnation. There is life in movement. India should no more resist change. It must move and go forward.'

'I tell you, the police are worse than ever, now it's section 377 at any opportunity and they'll arrest you. I'm doing so many of these cases now. Unnatural offences they say. I suppose they mean anything that doesn't involve a man on top of a woman missionary style,' says Sadeeq. Such a typical lawyer, he only gets excited when talking about law or politics.

The Central Park in the middle of Connaught Place was the oldest cruising area in Delhi but the metro works had suspended those activities and the inner circle in front of the Volga restaurant was now the recognised replacement.

Not that I am here to cruise, not with my present company. I look at my watch, think about what I'm going to do next.

'Why don't you get involved Ashok?' asks Sadeeq.

'There's never any change,' I say. 'Even when they said it wasn't illegal anymore, we were still harassed.'

'How can you say that? Now we've gone back 153 years to a law brought in by the British. Something that these people conveniently forget when they say that homosexuality is a Western disease. Politics is life Ashok, you can't ignore it.'

I think of my father, of how he would have distributed leaflets condemning us all, condemning his own son. 'Achaa, you're right.' I hope that's the end of it.

'So will you join us, start campaigning?' asks Sadeeq.

'No,' I say as firmly as I can.

Mathew shakes his head, exchanges a look with Sadeeq to tell him that it is no good to press me further. I see Mathew tinkering with a cross around his neck and in an attempt to steer the conversation to something different I ask, 'Is that new?'

'It's from Sacred Heart. You know I have been going to services again. Every Sunday, actually.'

'Really, I thought that was just Christmas mass, you're going every week now?' I'm annoyed that I don't know about this. I should know; I'm his oldest friend in Delhi.

'Pope Francis is different. He doesn't condemn gays and he's even said that he wants to look into why there are so many gay marriages.'

I'm not convinced. I remember six years ago when Mathew first arrived in Delhi. He told me how as a boy growing up in Kerala he had been a good Catholic and of how he had even felt the calling of priesthood. But although he had not yet acted on it, he was tormented by thoughts of men. He summoned up the bravery to discuss the issue with his priest. The Father assured him that it was a solemn sin to even think such things but with strength of purpose he could turn himself around and even enter the priesthood in time. All he needed to do was to re-orientate, to get some straight porn. He should watch that every day and night and most importantly whenever any thoughts of men came to him. When I had asked Mathew whether he tried to turn himself straight he did not answer. But he did tell me that soon after this he decided to leave Kerala, his family and abandon any thoughts of becoming a priest. I think of reminding Mathew of all this, but I hold my tongue. I already feel that he is becoming more distant from me; he has Sadeeq now.

Mathew delivers a piece of sweet potato chaat into Sadeeq's open mouth. They are just like a pair of newlyweds even though they've been together for a couple of years now. Sadeeq might be a lawyer but otherwise he's nothing special. Mathew lifts a finger to wipe away a smudge of brown from Sadeeq's mouth and proceeds to lick it. I am so embarrassed I have to look away.

'Good imli,' says Mathew. 'I wish you could get the sweet potato chaat all year long.'

Not for the first time I notice that Mathew is putting on weight and he doesn't seem to care. I've had enough of this. I get up and brush the crumbs off my jeans, crush the Thums Up cola can to announce my departure. 'I'm off to have some fun', I say.

'Where to?' asks Mathew.

'I don't know, I thought Janak Puri, maybe India Gate Lawns.'

'Do you want us to come with you?' Mathew asks half-heartedly.

'No, that's ok.'

'Well, if you're sure. Be careful though, especially if you go to the lawns, there are too many rough army types,' says Mathew.

'Just how I like them,' I say over my shoulder.

'I mean it Ashok, be careful.'

I catch his look of concern but then in the next moment he has his hand around the back of Sadeeq's head. I am already walking away from them. I decide to make my way to the lawns. If I catch a three-wheeler from the main stand I will get there by nine.

The traffic is gridlocked so by the time the driver lets me off at Rajpath Avenue it's well after nine. But that's good, as although there are still a few hawkers selling street food, bright toys and balloons, mainly the families with children have long gone home by now. India Gate stands high besides the lawns. The eternal flame, which flickers in the light breeze is flanked by uniformed soldiers. And near the flame on a pedestal stands the tribute of a shining rifle with a helmet resting upon it. Already, I spot some army types, perhaps real or just playing at being soldiers. And there are men like me too, dancing around the edges, waiting for a sign, the right look or hand gesture.

I begin a slow walk along the lawns as though I have all the time in the world. Then I see him. He has a soldier's bold upturned moustache that looks comical on someone who otherwise appears quite young. The man smiles at me, a mischievous kind of smile, lopsided as though he has something very interesting in mind. Not bad, but would he pay? The key was not to discuss money too early, not to shatter any illusion of flattery and chase. But also not too late to ignite an angry refusal that might turn nasty.

He's stopped and taken out a cigarette and then a lighter but he's waiting. I make my way through the lush grass, towards him. All the time, he is looking at me with that lopsided smile of his. As I near, I see that he has crease lines on his forehead and he is older than I first thought, perhaps mid -thirties. Now, he lights the two cigarettes that he has in his hand and holds one out to me. His hand is steady; I think that he must have done this many times before. I take the cigarette and put it to my lips. And I move to his side so that we are both looking out over the lawns, back towards the glow of India Gate.

'Nice evening, best time of the year to be here, not too hot, not too cold,' I say.

He doesn't reply, just takes another drag of his cigarette. I move closer to him and whisper in his ear, 'Do you want to go somewhere?'

He doesn't look at me but takes his barely smoked cigarette and throws it on the ground. He nods and starts walking away from me. Then he turns around towards me, 'You coming?' he asks.

I walk behind him. Maybe he's going towards the trees, an obvious choice. But then he veers off to the right and I see that he's going towards the men's toilets. 'Hold on,' I say. 'I don't like to go there.' Why would I? That was a place for free anonymous gropes. I put a hand on his shoulder. 'No, I said I don't like to go there. I can take you somewhere else.'

'Ok, ok, just wait for me here then, I have to go.' There is a hint of irritation in his voice. He carries on walking towards the toilets. He could have just as easily gone in the bushes.

I notice another man comes out from the side of the toilets. This one nods at the soldier then looks at me. I start retreating back. I am walking quickly, preparing to run. One of them has me by the shoulder and he kicks my legs. I fall to the ground.

I wonder whether the blood will wash from my best jeans. I'm sitting on the floor of a police cell. It reeks of stale urine. The floor and walls are decorated with yellowed streaks and crusts of dried vomit. I had been taken to a police van and bundled in with two other men. While I was waiting, I managed to get through to Mathew on my mobile phone. I told him that the police were taking me and I said other things that I would rather not think about now. I think I heard Mathew's voice but then one of the officers came round, hit the side of my face and took my mobile phone from me.

I'm relieved that it is the others that have been taken from the cell but I know that it will be my turn too soon, when I will be humiliated under the looming threat of sodomisation with a broom handle.

'Why are you doing this?' I asked them as if it was not obvious.

'Section 377 of the Indian Penal Code, it is an offence to engage in unnatural acts…'

I cover my ears to block out the men's cries and the laughter of the police. I want to call for my mother. Doesn't anyone call for their mother when they are this terrified? I think about when I last spoke to her, two years ago.

'Ashok, my prayers are answered. How are you beta?'

'I'm well Maa, I'm still working in the call centre.' It was so good to hear her voice. 'I'd like to come and see you Maa.'

'Yes, beta you come home. It doesn't matter that you didn't finish your education. You can come and work in the shop and we will find you a nice girl to marry.'

'Maa…nothing has changed…I'm still not interested in girls.' I still could not quite say it, that I was gay and that it would be as easy to change that as to change the colour of my eyes from brown to green.

'You know your father is doing very well now with the BJP. He will be standing as a candidate soon. You do understand, don't you Ashok? Come home, but only when you are ready to settle down and marry.'

No, it's not my mother I call for but 'Mathew,' again and again until I fall asleep exhausted on the concrete floor.

I am startled from my sleep and for a moment think that I've just had a very bad dream. An older officer stands before me and there are the two others behind him. It takes me a few minutes to focus. The older one is wearing a peak cap, and he is holding something in his hand. He has it in the air, hesitates and then brings the stick down hard upon my head.

They take me to another room. Someone tells me how much fun I will have with the Inspector; he can't stand homosexuals. My stomach feels like it has been turned inside out and I hold back from retching.

'Sorry, that I had to do that, be rough like that. They were watching. Sorry that it's on your face.' The Inspector moves towards the door and locks it. He tells me to sit down and pulls out the seat from behind the table, placing it next to mine.

I trace the large bruise on my head with a shaking finger. Then I recognise him. What was his chat up line? 'Are you an Aries or Sagittarius?' I was neither. What I said was,

'You're right; I'm an Aries.' I would be whatever he wanted me to be that night.

A few months back, it was the Moonlight Club in Kailash Colony. They were playing a mix of hip hop, R & B and a few old Hindi hits. I yearned for some Kylie, any Bollywood this side of the decade. Then by some miracle, the DJ put on 'Kajra re'. There was a cheer and everyone was a diva shaking their hips so that the dance floor was at once crowded. I knew that there would be men at the side looking at me, admiring me, thinking that they might have a chance. If I didn't get some work tonight then it would at least be pleasure.

That was when I saw him. He was wearing a dark safari suit, thick tufts of hair all over his arms, spilling out of his open collar. And he was staring at me; he couldn't stop.

'Do you want to dance?' I asked. The man was nervous. I put out a hand and he took it but instead of holding it, he shook it firmly. He was a clumsy dancer, an over-sized toddler who couldn't quite keep to the beat. I leant in closer to him. 'Do you want to go somewhere else?' The music was too loud. 'I said, do you want to go to my place?' I caught a glimpse of his expensive watch. He must know that he would have to pay, nothing this good would be free to a man like him.

The Inspector gets up and crouches down behind me. He reaches an arm around my waist so that he has his head nestled in the small of my back.

'You are so beautiful,' he says muffling the words into my back. 'So very beautiful.'

My shirt is wet. I can't quite make out if it's tears or sweat from his large head. He is murmuring still, sobbing too, 'Why can't I control myself?'

I pull myself away from his grasp, try to keep composed. 'Let me pour you a drink, whisky? You must have some, where is it?' I ask. He smells and acts as though he must have had quite a few drinks already.

'In the top drawer,' he tells me.

On the desk there is a picture of his wife and two boys in their school uniforms. Smart boys with matching side partings, the kind of boys any father would be proud of. When I open the drawer I see a bottle of Johnny Walker, it must have been an expensive bribe. And there is something metal too, a policeman's pistol.

Now I will have to show my gratitude. I wet my lips with my tongue, feel dried blood where a fist or foot has caught me. I think of the gun, of how I could take it and shoot, but my hands shake too much and besides which, I have never killed a man. So I close the drawer and pour a drink for the Inspector. There's a knock on the door.

'I'm busy with the suspect,' says the Inspector.

'Sorry Inspector Saab, but it can't wait.'

The Inspector goes to the door, opens it just wide enough to speak to the officer. Then he's gone. The officer comes in and roughly pulls me up from the chair and takes me out, back to the cell.

I sit on the hard floor of the cell, head bowed down, clutching my knees close to me so that I have become something small; something less than a man. When I look up I see the officer is back. I don't move, keeping my arms around me, bracing myself for another round of blows. But it doesn't come. Instead, he tells me to get a move on and to get my things from the front desk.

At the desk, I pick up my wallet. The collection of five hundred rupee notes and my mobile phone have gone. When I look through the window I see Sadeeq with one hand hooked in this flowing advocate's robes. He's speaking to a police officer, pointing his other hand back towards me. I should be happy to see him, relieved that he's here to help me but I am strangely deflated.

As I go out of the station, Sadeeq nods at me and waves me on while he continues speaking to the officer. I walk on to the road and that's when I see him. He's looking down, frowning. My heartbeat quickens. I don't have to call him; he lifts his eyes to mine and doesn't look away. I remember what I had said to Mathew in the call, when I asked him to come for me. The words I would not normally have spoken, that I loved him.

The Swim
JAMILAH AHMED

The perimeter walls of the American Compound were at odds with the rest of the city of Dubai. The stone was dark. It had been selected to stand out against the soft desert background. The houses here had sloping roofs and small chimney outlets, which had no function beyond the decorative. Sand gathered in the crevices, and solidified into salted crusts. At their coffee-mornings, American housewives would swap tips on how best to combat this problem, and discuss how their maid or gardener could keep the exterior tidy. They hadn't considered removing these unnecessary appendages.

Ameera liked having a friend who lived on the American compound. On days spent at Christine's house, she lived an expat life, and stepped outside her own family ways. Leah pulled up outside the house, and Ameera ran in, saying hello to Christine's mother as she made her way to Christine's room. The bedroom had posters of boy-bands on the walls with 'I love A-Ha' written in black marker, and kisses in smudged red lipstick. As Def Leppard or Bon Jovi shouted from the speakers, Christine would tell Ameera of the latest development in her love life. There were several boys on the compound with whom she was allowed to go on dates. These dates were sanctioned by Christine's parents as long as they remained within the walls of the compound.

14

Recently however, Christine had grown fascinated by the US marines who were invited into the compound on 'home-visits'. Both girls knew that this transgression could have serious consequences. Ameera wondered if everyone was pushing at the boundaries of their worlds, asking to be let into another place, if only for a while.

Christine began to load blue eye shadow onto her lids, puffs of it floated down to the desk. She wore a bright yellow pencil skirt and a loose black t-shirt that slipped off one shoulder, revealing a blue bra-strap. Ameera looked down at her own skirt, soft pink with a paisley print, that flowed down to her toes, in their flat black shoes. Her outfit had pleased her this morning, now she felt out-of-place, like an extra from *Little House on the Prairie*. Christine's hair was hard with hairspray, and Ameera realised there must already be a plan for the day. Christine shut the door and jumped cross-legged onto the bed beside Ameera, 'Do you want to meet Serge today? Come for a bit, and then let us have some time to be alone?'

Ameera stared at the blue eyes. She had no interest in meeting this latest crush of Christine's, but wanted even less to be on her own, while Christine spent time alone with a marine officer. Christine carried on, 'There's a BBQ we can go to, and you might meet someone there too. Then Serge has said he wants us to be alone! Can you believe that? He wants me!'

Ameera felt repulsed, she didn't think she could bear to meet this American man who said such things to her friend.

Sometimes Ameera thought nothing happened, sometimes she believed Christine's tales of body-to-body exploration. She looked blankly at Christine, 'I don't want to meet anyone, I will come for the BBQ so I know where you are. But this isn't a good idea. It's going too far.'

Christine hugged her knees to her chest, her make-up smudged as her eyes crinkled with excitement, 'I can't believe he's chosen me! It's the best summer of my life!'

Ameera picked at the cookies left for them by Christine's mother. This was not the best summer of her life. She did not want a world in which everyone grabbed at what was outside their reach. Maybe her father was right, maybe it was better when things stayed the same, in their 'proper places'. But such phrases belonged to another time, they held no power now. Christine offered her the eye shadow brush, 'Shall we get ready?'

Ameera took the powder and dabbed some around her lashes. The blue looked ridiculous around her dark brown eyes, and she rubbed it off quickly. She found a black eye-pencil in Christine's make-up bag and drew hard lines around her eyes that smeared into the corners. She looked at herself through half-closed lids, sideways on. She looked different from when she had arrived, older. She would not have been allowed to leave her own house with such make-up. Ameera took a bottle of bright red nail-varnish from another small zipped bag. The gloss hardened and dried, transforming her hands into someone else's. She would have to take it off before she went home.

When Christine was ready they went to tell her mother they were going out.

'How's your mum Ameera? She didn't stop for a chat when she dropped you off this morning, which was a shame. Is she well?' Sheila often asked Ameera's mother in for a coffee, or spent half an hour outside in the sun, leaning into the car as they talked. Christine prodded Ameera impatiently, she replied quickly 'Yes, thanks, she's fine.'

'And you? How are you? I thought you did very well at the Inauguration Ceremony you know. That's a lot to take on, a recital and playing in the orchestra I thought you managed very well.'

Ameera didn't know what to say to this, clearly she had not managed well but gave the answer she felt Sheila wanted, 'It was OK, I'll practise more another time.'

'Don't you worry about it petal, I'm sure your mum and dad are proud of you.'

Ameera pushed her face into a smile and followed Christine out into the sun.

As they walked, Christine recounted her conversation with Serge the previous evening, adding details that left Ameera increasingly less enthusiastic about the afternoon ahead. They neared the clubhouse and were spotted by the hostess, Christine's neighbour Martha. A short wide woman with a helmet of dyed black hair, who bowled over and engulfed them in a hug, 'Girls, I am pleased you're here! We're about to light the fire and you can help Billy and Chuck!' She laughed loudly as if a funny joke had been shared, and ushered them towards her son and his friend. Behind them, Serge leaned against the wall, his tall frame casting shadows on the pool surface. As they talked to the boys, Serge walked over and asked Billy if he needed help with the BBQ and so the game began. Christine and Serge were the leaders in this dance, and Ameera and the two teenage boys mere buffers between the couple and the adults. It was sad, thought Ameera, that Martha could not read the dynamics of this group, was not alert to the role of her own son as pawn in an elaborate game.

When they all sat down to lunch, the dynamic abated slightly. Christine was irritable now that she was no longer the focus of Serge's attention. She hardly spoke to Ameera and they ate at each other's sides in silence as the adults talked around them. Serge talked of his weekend leave spent at Martha's house, how the time spent in a family home gave him renewed vigour once he was back on the base ship. Ameera wondered how many others were on the ship, how many naval officers came ashore and meddled in lives before they disappeared, literally, into the horizon. She was worried about the afternoon he and Christine had planned. He had nothing to lose. He did not belong here, the rules did not hold his world together. She watched Christine, her laughs louder at his jokes than anyone else's, her wonder writ large on her face.

After lunch they headed into the clubhouse café for ice-creams, and Serge suggested a walk down to the beach. Ameera knew this was her cue, even before Christine's blue beacons signalled this was her moment. The boys turned towards the pier in search of new playmates and Ameera said bye to Christine and Serge, who walked away, towards the far end of the beach.

Ameera sat at the ice-cream bar. She had hoped that a day spent with Christine would rid her of her thoughts, not leave her alone with them. She tried to think how to occupy the next two hours, until Christine returned, and they could go home again. The shop had filled up now, groups of friends milling around looking for ice-cream and entertainment. Ameera watched them, and listened to their jokes and banter. Her ice-cream finished, she bent down to reach for her bag, but her elbow brushed into the man next to her, a smudge of his bright pink ice-cream glowed on her arm.

'I'm sorry, here have my napkin.' He wasn't American, he smiled but knew to look away, not to embarrass her with too long a gaze. Ameera took the napkin and mumbled her thanks as she walked quickly out of the shop. She started walking away from the crowds and was about to throw the napkin into the bin when she noticed a scrawl on the edge of it. A shot of recognition trilled through her body. She had always discarded such notes quickly in the past, as if holding them for too long would taint her. Today, alone, she read it carefully: 'Deen 0770 347457 call me'. She scrunched the napkin quickly into her hand and kept walking, past the bin. She looked down into her hand, and read it again, as if the ink might have faded in the few minutes. She didn't look back, but pushed the napkin in to her bag and zipped it shut. She walked on until she reached the end of the compound, the rusted metal fence stretching out to sea.

She was away from everyone now, only a lone swimmer at the periphery of her vision to distract her. She didn't know if his splashes were bravado or the inelegance of a poor swimmer. I could do better than that, thought Ameera. She looked back along the empty stretch of beach, the pier was far away and she could not tell if the small dots that moved back and forth were men or women. They would not be able to tell who she was. She stepped out of her long skirt, and unbuttoned her shirt. Ameera stood on the beach, in her black vest and long black leggings that she wore beneath for modesty. She wondered if from a distance she could pass for a scuba-diver. She smiled, imagining a new trend in swimwear for local women. Ameera felt her face twist in amusement, the movement seemed from a long time ago.

She walked forward into the sea until it reached her armpits, and she could hardly see the bright red nail varnish on her toes. She ducked under the water, and let herself sink almost to the bottom, around her tiny fish burrowed into the sand, alarmed at this invader from above. She pushed upwards and took in a big gulp of air. As she wiped the salt-water out of her eyes, and pushed her hair back, Serge's face came into focus, it refused to leave her thoughts. She ducked back under the water and continued to swim, came up for air and then disappeared again as she followed the line of the fence beneath the sea. Every time the face reappeared she ducked under the water again, until it came to her no longer. She swam on, leaving the end of the barrier behind as it dipped beneath the surface. She could swim out of the compound if she wanted.

The water was cooler now that she was further from the shore. Far out, on the right, the naval ship hovered on the horizon, a small dash against the clear sky. Her limbs began to ache as she swam into the waves. To her left Ameera could make out the pier. She had no idea what time it was. She swivelled round in the water. She floated onto her back and let the sun dazzle her eyes as she squinted upwards. Her feet and hands paddled gently as she absorbed the sounds and sensations of being surrounded by water. A sense of peace crept into her, it filled her entirety and pushed out, at last, the turmoil of the past few weeks. She stared up at the sky, Christine, Serge, her squabbling sisters, and even her father all seemed tiny and distant.

Out here, she was more alone than she had ever experienced. She flipped over onto her belly, legs straight and her heels dipped up and down with the tide. No-one could see her. If she put her mouth and nose into the water, she could eliminate the shore from her vision. Wave after wave tipped over her and towards the beach. Ameera let her body sink into the water, and felt the sea lap over her face, like a blind drawn down over her face, it closed off the means to talk, to listen, to discover. She wondered how long it would take before they would notice she was gone, how long it would take before her limbs could float no more.

Ninety Days
ASHOK PATEL

Mahesh looked around his shop with sadness, like a General counting the cost of defeat. His hair, usually carefully groomed in a Shammi Kapoor hair style, was unusually dishevelled, and he hadn't shaved for two days. He wore a wide collared shirt, and tight fitting creased trousers, both tailored in far-off Bombay and bought in Uganda from a shop three doors away. The Priest suspected that Mahesh had not left his shop since they last spoke the day before.

'Father, take the TV, that radio and those kettles,' he said, pointing to some shelves.

'Thank you, my friend. We'll make good use of them,' the Priest said. He placed a hand gently on Mahesh's shoulder, knowing that there was little he could say at this point to make him feel better.

'My father started this business thirty years ago and I've run it for the last ten. We've built a good reputation. People have heard of us in Jinja and even in Kampala,' Mahesh said. The Priest nodded in agreement.

'I had such big plans for this business. The other radio and that typewriter can go to the Sister at the Madira Blind School.'

'I'll make sure she gets them.'

'I've given Freddie and my fundis the things they wanted. They've been good workers,' Mahesh said. 'I was wiring a

Catholic Church near Meroto, when an Italian doctor came to tell me the news.'

'I heard Amin's speech that day on the radio. I couldn't believe my ears' the Priest said. Both men stepped outside on to the street. Mahesh stared at the large sign at the front of the shop Vasani Electric Service for a long time. 'Now gangs of young men, full of beer, come round here hurling insults and threats at the Asian businesses,' Mahesh said. The priest shook his head in disbelief. Mahesh breathed deeply, locked the shop door and handed the keys to the Priest. He looked up and down the unusually deserted main street of Soroti.

'Even as I was closing down my business, I didn't really believe that he would go through with it.' Mahesh looked at his shop for the last time. 'Every day I kept hoping he would change his mind. But he didn't.'

'Thank you for all your donations and help to the Mission over the years. We'll miss you,' the Priest said. Mahesh held him tightly, fighting off waves of emotion, as they embraced for the last time.

'I should have taken my family out of here months ago.'

'Nobody knew it would come to this.'

'What did we do wrong Father?' Mahesh asked, blinking out a teardrop from his left eye, which meandered down his face before crashing into his moustache.

'You can't blame yourself,' the Priest said. He wanted to say more, but from the corner of his eye he glimpsed three armed soldiers who had appeared at the end of the street.

The Priest noted the quickening pace of the oncoming soldiers and pulled away. 'Don't think badly of all Africans my friend. May God be with you and your family.' Mahesh eyed the soldiers and nodded.

'Ring me at the Mission if I can help you,' the Priest whispered, as the sweat on his face made his smooth black skin glisten in the afternoon sun. He turned quickly towards the soldiers.

'Kukomesha! Kukomesha!' one of the soldiers shouted 'Muenda, kukomesha!' Another soldier pointed his gun in the direction of the slight Indian man getting into his car. The Priest walked towards them, shielding his friend with outspread arms and a smile. Mahesh sped away, taking the first turning off the main street, with the looming Soroti Rock on his right. As he turned, he fleetingly glimpsed, in his rear view mirror, the soldiers shouting and gesticulating as they approached the Priest. The familiar sight of the Rock calmed him. Images of countless family picnics in its shadow flew by. One in particular lingered for a while; him drinking from a cold bottle of Eagle beer and chattering to his wife, as they watched their children playing happily.

He drove his car into the compound of his bungalow, in the Asian Quarter of Soroti. There was an eerie silence around the Society, which was composed of a cluster of bungalows with adjoining yards. Children would normally be playing noisily outside and people talking loudly in Gujarati from their porches. Hindu, Sikh and Muslim families all lived here, constantly in and out of each other's houses, sharing food and helping each other. Their lives had coalesced over several generations, firmly rooted in their shared values. Many had fathers and grandfathers who had come from India to work on the railways in Uganda. They realised there was opportunity here and had gradually moved into business. They started as shopkeepers, dukawallahs, now often used as a term of insult by Africans. Mahesh remembered how the Asians and Africans had danced together in the streets, when General Amin had ousted President Obote nearly two years earlier, in January 1971. Now, most of the bungalows in the Society were empty. Just a few Asian families had hung on, clinging to life in a country where they were not wanted. The irony of it all, somehow allowed a smile to stumble on to his face. His wife, Lina, was placing a tower of chapattis on the table, when he entered the house. She threw him a thunderous glare which instantly dissipated the smile on his face. She was a tiny woman, with an unusually fair complexion, and dressed in a plain cotton sari. She turned stiffly, her slim frame awash with anger, and walked into the kitchen.

Mahesh took off his shoes, and nudged them on to the end of a neat line of shoes and champals idling next to the doorway. He stopped momentarily as he caught sight of his reflection in a mirror on the wall, next to a photo of Mahatma Gandhi, and images of Ganesh and Hanuman.

'Maheshbhai is a green chilli of a man,' people said of him. He revelled in his reputation, taking over the business from his father when he had retired to India and keeping a tight rein on it. He understood the value of goodwill and had nurtured his customers. People respected him and he had often been invited to events with politicians and dignitaries. He had built a good life for his family in this country, the Pearl of Africa. He shuffled over to the dining table and curled into a chair. The house was quiet, but he knew both his children would be awake in their room, whispering themselves to sleep with stories full of truths and untruths. Over dinner recently, six year old Anita had asked 'why do they hate us daddy?'

'Because they're karyas, and they're stupid,' her ten year old brother Sanjay had replied.

'But why do we have to leave? We're more important than they are. Why can't they leave?' she had asked. Anita and her brother had laughed loudly, until their mother had arched her eyebrows into a near perfect inverted VV shape and silenced them.

'The karyas are angry because of what the Asians have. They're jealous,' Mahesh had explained to them.

'Maybe the Africans are angry because of what the Asians won't let them have,' his wife had suggested. They all ate the rest of their dinner in silence.

Lina returned from the kitchen with a pot of spicy daal and rice heaped in a bowl. She carefully arranged the rice, chapattis, daal, matoke shak, chilli mogo, papad, onion salad and pickles on the table, like an artist planning a canvas.

'I haven't been sending them to school,' she said.

'We leave early tomorrow,' her husband said.

'Three houses in the Society got broken into last week. They terrified the families and took money, jewellery, even some furniture.'

'I've arranged for a car and driver to come here in the morning. I'll get visas in Kampala.'

'Why didn't we leave months ago like a lot of the other families?' she demanded.

'I didn't think it would come to this' he murmured.

'Freddie says that lots of Africans are disappearing, especially in Kampala,' she said as Mahesh chewed his food joylessly.

'Bodies are found dumped in the forests and rivers every day. Didn't you think it was time to go?' she asked.

'It's karyas killing karyas, nothing to do with us. It's tribal, you know what they're like. Amin's thugs are running wild.'

'Couldn't you see the Society emptying out? You had to wait until he orders us to leave, before you think about your family's safety?'

'I said we're leaving tomorrow!' Mahesh said. The sound of the youngest crying filtered through into the lounge.

'He gave us ninety days to get out. That was nearly two months ago!' she said as she got up from the table.

'You didn't have to finish all the jobs before closing the business. You left us alone here,' she said walking away from him. Then she turned to him, her lips like two pencil lines. He lowered his eyes to shield himself.

'Where is your precious business now?' she said.

Mahesh sat on the porch, intently watching the African sun setting, bringing with it the promise of night. He shut his eyes and enjoyed the cool breeze playing on his skin. The sound of approaching footsteps made him open his eyes, and he smiled at the welcome sight of his friend Anil. The Society children all called him the Laughing Uncle. Anil enjoyed laughing, and enjoyed making others laugh even more. He was a big man, not tall, with a habit of moving his head from side to side when talking. When he laughed his ample girth undulated up and down, whilst his double chin wobbled left and right, like unruly bullocks pulling a cart. But Anil's laughter had not clattered around the Society for many weeks now. Mahesh hadn't seen Anil for a while and noticed that he'd lost a lot of weight and his shiny black hair had started to grey. The two men shook hands and watched the sunset in silence.

'My parents are in India now at my sister's house' said Anil, finally breaking the silence. Mahesh smiled 'Good. What about you?'

'They want me to join them. But I think I'll stay,' Anil replied.

'I don't want to leave either,' Mahesh said. 'But it's safer for the family to go'.

'I don't know where I'd go,' Anil said. 'This is my home.'

'We're leaving tomorrow morning Anil.'

'Where to?'

'We have relatives in the UK, but we need visas. Getting to Kampala won't be easy. There are Army checkpoints everywhere.'

'I heard something really bad today,' Anil said hesitantly.

'What?'

'You know some Asians have been trying to get to Kenya by train?' Anil continued. 'Ugandan soldiers have been stopping the trains near the Kenyan border, looking for money and jewellery. But two Asian men got into an argument with them and the soldiers beat them up. Then they raped their wives.'

'My God!' Mahesh said.

'Some of the karyas on the train were cheering the soldiers on,' Anil said.

The sounds of the African night crowded them. They were suddenly more aware of the constant chirping of crickets, and the distant barking of quarrelsome dogs. Mahesh went in to the house and came back with a bottle of Johnnie Walker and two glasses. He poured whisky into the glasses and both men took a sip.

'My father told me that when Asians first came to Uganda, there wasn't even a currency here. So they used the Indian rupee,' Mahesh said.

'Why is he doing this?' Anil asked.

'Who knows? Amin's thugs have slaughtered thousands and everyone is terrified. Inflation is high and the poor can't afford to buy food. He knows he's not popular' Mahesh said. 'Suddenly he has a dream and God tells him to kick all the Asians out of Uganda.'

'Now they're singing his name on the streets. They say he's doing this because an Asian woman he wanted as his fourth wife rejected him,' Anil said.

'Who knows? They all want Asian women to marry black men. Even Obote used to go on about that.' Mahesh said. They stare into the blackness of the African night. Eventually, Anil got up and both men shook hands solemnly.

'Send me a postcard of Buckingham Palace,' Anil said with a smile and with that the Laughing Uncle disappeared into the night.

Mahesh awoke to the noises of a bustling house, still under the blanket of night. He got ready quickly and entered the lounge to find that Lina had been giving away furniture and kitchen utensils. Dembe, the girl who had helped her in the kitchen for many years, had brought her family and they were taking whatever they wanted. The children were both ready and sitting on a sofa against the wall. Sanjay was awake, red-eyed and bewildered, whilst Anita slept with her head on his arm. Mahesh went outside to find Freddie waiting, with four fundis, mostly electricians and carpenters that he had employed regularly for years. Freddie had started working for the family before Mahesh was born and though in his sixties, was still a sprightly man. He was the best electrician in Soroti and all the fundis respected him.

'Freddie, you need anything from the house?' Mahesh asked.

'Thank you Bwana. Mama has already given us many things,' Freddie replied, his eyes moistening. Lina's voice drifted out from the house, calling for Freddie, and he responded immediately.

The headlights from a car pierced the night, as it entered the compound, closely followed by another one. Mahesh's friend, Chotu got out of the first car.

'Jai Shree Krishna,' Chotu said.

'Jai Shree Krishna Chotu,' Mahesh replied. A young African man got out of the second car and joined them.

'This is Mugaba, Mahesh.' Chotu told him. The men nodded at each other.

'I trust him. He'll drive you to Kampala and then to the Airport,' Chotu said and slapped Mugaba on the back, triggering a big grin on his face. Mahesh handed Mugaba a bank draft for 20,000 shillings. Mugaba concealed it in a compartment underneath the driver's car seat, behind a metal plate which he screwed in. Mahesh also gave him 500 shillings in notes, which disappeared into the hem of Mugaba's pants.

'Get out safely,' Chotu said as he got into his car.

'With God's help,' Mahesh replied. 'What about you and the family?'

'Relatives in America. Got the visas yesterday,' he said punching the air. Mahesh smiled and waved as Chotu drove off.

Freddie placed their luggage in the car boot, whilst Lina got the children into the back. Dembe had already started crying in the house, and when the time came to say goodbye, she was inconsolable. Lina tearfully hugged her, and remembered that there were some jars of Ponds moisturising cream in the bedroom dresser that she could take. Mahesh and Lina hugged Freddie and thanked him for his service to the family. Mahesh pressed the house keys into Freddie's hands.

'If you can keep the house from Amin's people, be happy in it with your family,' Mahesh told him. Freddie wept uncontrollably. Mahesh hugged each one of the fundis, and gave his car keys to the oldest one.

'Sell it, and split the money between you,' he told him. Lina got in the back of the car with the children, as Mahesh got in the front with the driver. They waved a final goodbye as the car pulled out of the compound. Mahesh and Lina knew that the Africans were crying not just because of the bond that had been built between them and the Vasani family over the years, but also because they were all losing their livelihoods. The Asians and their African workers were all entering an uncertain future.

Dawn broke as they left Soroti, and Mahesh could see Crowned cranes in the fields next to the narrow straight road. He smiled as he watched the male birds doing funny little dances to attract females. No wonder, he thought, that this majestic bird was on the national flag of Uganda. He looked over at Lina and caught her smiling as she watched the birds too.

'Bwana,' Mugaba whispered as he gestured with his fingers to the other side of the road. Mahesh saw the drooping body of young black woman tied to a tree by the waist with rope. She had a gaping gunshot hole in her head. He glanced at the back, thankful that Lina was still looking at the birds on the other side and both children were asleep.

It wasn't long before they came across a checkpoint manned by three soldiers and a couple of policemen. As the car slowed down Mahesh recognised one of them.

'Jambo, jambo,' he waved at him enthusiastically. 'Harbari gani?'

The policeman recognised Mahesh and after a few words with the others, waved the car on. Mahesh looked at Mugaba with raised eyebrows. They both knew that their luck couldn't last. To their surprise, the next two checkpoints were equally trouble free. But at the check points at Kumi and Mbale the soldiers opened all their suitcases, rifled through the contents and took whatever they wanted. They searched Mahesh, poked around the car, and made Lina and the children empty their pockets. The soldiers perceived Mugaba to be a naive and harmless village boy and he rarely got out the car. That evening they queued for three hours at the next check point at Owen Falls Bridge. The soldiers were all drunk. 'Out the car, you bloodsucker,' one shouted at Mahesh. They spread-eagled him on the ground and searched him. Another put his foot on the back of his neck, and shoved a rifle into his head. 'Dukawallah, you have milked this country dry and given nothing back. I will kill you right now!' he shouted.

'We're leaving Uganda. We're leaving,' Mahesh said.

Inside the car, Lina was distraught, convinced that her husband was going to be shot in front of her and tried to calm her children. Mugaba got out of the car. 'Here,' he said, holding out a 100 shilling note to the soldier pinning Mahesh down. The soldier's eyes narrowed. 'Where did you get that village boy?' he hissed.

'He gave it to me,' Mugaba replied wide eyed and pointing to Mahesh.

'They use you, pay you shit. Why do you help them?' he asked. 'Where's the rest?'

'That's it, that's all he gave me' Mugaba said.

'Search him and the car,' the soldier barked. Mugaba and the car were searched, but they found nothing. Sensing that there might be greater pickings in the other cars in the queue, they let Mahesh get up.

'We want our country back you bloodsucker,' the soldier said and slammed the butt of his rifle into Mahesh's face as he got into the car. Mugaba drove off, as the soldiers laughed, shooting their rifles into the air.

'Where did you hide the money?' Mahesh asked Mugaba, as he wiped the blood off his face. 'Better you don't know' Mugaba replied with a smile.

'How's the nose?' Lina asked. 'Broken, I think.' Mahesh replied.

'Don't wipe all the blood off. They might take pity on you at the next check point,' Mugaba said.

'How can they call us bloodsuckers?' Mahesh said.

'They don't understand Mahesh. Forget it,' Lina said gently, wondering what had hurt her husband more, the blow to his face or the insults.

'Maybe they'll realise what we've done for Uganda one day,' Mahesh said wiping blood off his hands. Mahesh wondered how Africans and Asians could have lived side by side for so long and yet be apart.

'In my village we have a saying, Bwana; a dog with a bone in his mouth cannot bite you. Dada Amin gives his soldiers plenty of food, beer and whisky I hear.' There were two more check points before Kampala, neither were as bad as Owen Falls Bridge, and Mugaba used the rest of the money to bribe the soldiers. They arrived in Kampala tired and hungry, having taken 30 hours to cover the 290 km from Soroti.

Mahesh, Lina and the children all felt so much better after a meal and a good night's rest. They stayed with a family friend, Nathu, in his beautiful home in an affluent suburb of Kampala. At breakfast, they were served by uniformed servants at an enormous dining table. Mahesh had heard that Nathu and his brother owned a shopping centre in Kampala.

'Thank you for letting us stay Nathubhai,' Mahesh said.

'No need to say thank you, we've known your father for years. Stay as long as you want,' Nathu replied. 'My family are all in the UK now and I'm leaving to join them in two days.'

'Really. What will happen to your house and business?' Mahesh asked.

'They're worthless. The banks have stopped all business transactions. Nobody wants to pay good money for anything Asians own, knowing that we're being forced to leave,' Nathu said. 'We've always had African partners and we've transferred the businesses to them. Whether they stay loyal to us or not in years to come, is anyone's guess.' Mahesh and Lina looked at each other, shocked at Nathu's nonchalance.

'I'm sorry,' said Mahesh, not knowing what else to say.

'Don't be, we're all in the same boat' Nathu said. 'My family is safe. We'll start again in the UK.'

'What did we do wrong Nathubhai?' Mahesh asked.

'You know the Africans say that if you have a snake and an Indian in front of you, kill the Indian' Nathu said. 'They don't trust us, and we don't respect them. Maybe we should have respected the Africans more. Maybe we should have taken less and given more.'

'But, surely we don't deserve this?' Mahesh asked.

'No,' Nathu said. 'We don't deserve this. You get your visas and get your family out of here.'

Mahesh and Lina waited outside the British High Commission with thousands of others, many of them having slept outside on the road overnight. Eventually after queuing for eight hours, they were seen and after some form filling were asked to come back two days later. They queued again two days later, this time with their children, and were interviewed after a five hour wait. There were a lot more questions and a lot more form filling. Three days later Mahesh went back and waited in the queue all day. He had got there very early, but there were still hundreds of people in the queue. When his turn came, he was overjoyed when he was handed visas to the UK for him and his family. He went with Mugaba to the Bank of Uganda and cashed the bank draft. They were fortunate and didn't get harassed by the armed soldiers prowling outside the bank. Mahesh then immediately went and bought tickets to the UK for his family for 14,000 shillings.

Nathu had said an emotional goodbye to his workers the day before. Mahesh and Lina had offered to stay somewhere else, but Nathu wouldn't hear of it. He had left some keys and instructions with Mahesh and had given him details of how to contact him in the UK. Mahesh secured the house and they all stayed together in the housekeeper's small room that night, as Nathu had suggested. They watched their children sleeping and listened to the sounds of Kampala at night as they held each other. Silence enveloped them as the city night sounds subsided and they waited for dawn to break. Then they heard some thuds and hammering, and their hearts pounded as they realised that the house was being broken into. Lina wrapped her arms round her children as Mahesh got up and stood by the door. They could hear people moving round the house and talking in Swahili.

'Lock the door after me,' Mahesh said.

'No, stay with us,' Lina said.

'Don't worry, Nathu told me what to do. Look after the children,' Mahesh said slipping out of the room. When he entered the lounge, there were five men in Ugandan Army uniforms there. One was sitting on a sofa, whilst the others were holding sub machine guns and searching the room.

'This is not my house,' Mahesh said looking at the soldier on the sofa.

'Where is Nathu Patel?' the soldier asked.

'He left Uganda yesterday,' Mahesh said. The soldier frowned and looked around the room. Mahesh went over to a cupboard and took out a bottle of Johnnie Walker and poured a glass. He gave the glass and the bottle to the soldier on the sofa.

'Foreign whisky,' he said with a smile before taking a sip. Mahesh took out a bag of keys from his pocket and handed it to him.

'Keys to the garage and two Mercedes cars,' Mahesh said. 'Take them. There's nothing else here.'

The soldier got up, handed the bottle of whisky to one of his men and walked up to Mahesh and stared at him with his bloodshot eyes.

'I have children. We are leaving Uganda tomorrow,' Mahesh said.

'Tell the Queen that Big Daddy says hello,' the soldier said and headed to the garage with his men.

Mugaba took them to Entebbe Airport the next morning, expertly bribing soldiers at each check point. Amin had allowed each family to take fifty British pounds as they left Uganda. Mahesh gave what was left in shillings to Mugaba, with heartfelt gratitude. He left them, as he had met them, with a big grin on his face.

As the plane took off, the passengers sighed with relief and then clapped with joy. Mahesh held on to Lina and his children, as the plane soared into the African sky. He wondered if he would ever set foot on the red soil of Uganda again and quietly cried for the country he loved.

'What will we do in the UK?' Lina asked.

'We'll start again,' Mahesh said and held his family tightly.

Red and Purple
JUHI THE FRAGRANT

In a corner of a small room, that might have once been painted a greyish blue colour, sits a transparent fish tank. Within it, separated by a sheet of black plastic, swim two fish. One—the colour of crushed jaba-kusum, the intensely blood-red flower, heaped onto all images of Maa Kali, and the other—the heady purple of the postu plant, the intoxicating opiate. Their tails and fins unfurl in the shimmering water and create the illusion of two dancing prima ballerinas giving a performance. These are two male Siamese fighting fishes.

Their master Rabin Roy stands nearby, staring at his face in the rusted mirror which hangs above, on the damp wall. The shock of hair that dominated his forehead has been shorn, and he recognises his dead mother's cone-shaped forehead reflected back at him. The tangled mess of eyebrows above his wide, round eyes, has been threaded to an angular perfection, and his moustache—lost.

His lips still look like a man's, swarthy and chapped. He picks up the lipstick kept on the large bed dominating the room, and uncaps it. His irises train on his lips, as they are smeared savagely with a metallic red-purple colour. His fingers still grip the brown plastic cylinder, as he searches for his face within the minuscule mirror.

The closed door crashes open and his wife Sharmila barges in, her eyes trained on her knobby fingers—busily counting currency notes. Rabin frowns.

'Ma has given money for new clothes for the children. I have taken it,' she says. 'Its a gift. For Pujo. They need new clothes for Pujo.' She finally raises her lowered eyes to look at her husband. Her eyes widen and her mouth falls open. She clutches the money more tightly in her hands. 'Wha ... what ... where ... ' her lips resemble the fishes'—opening and closing repeatedly.

Rabin takes a deep breath, and removes the dark barrier between the two fishes.

Sharmila's eyes dart around—between her husband's mysteriously hairless back, and the two fighting fish now sizing each other up, flaring their tails and circling each other. She bursts into hysterical laughter. With spit flying out, and still clutching the money to her chest, she says, 'Did you lose again? Was this part of the bet?'

'I am starting a new job today.' He says.

Mid-laugh, she stops and stares, her mouth still open. His metallic lips seem to mesmerise her. She looks away to watch the fish—one lunges, while the other feints and lunges back.

'New job? Why didn't you tell me? I will iron your good shirt. Wear that.' She says.

'I will not need the shirt.' He says. 'But, I would like your help in wearing this.' He picks up a bright red saree with a wide purple border from their bed.

Her kohl-lined eyes search his, for humour. Her neck stiff, she asks, 'Are you joking?'

His kohl-lined eyes remain serious.

Sharmila takes a step back, and searches for her hairy, bushy eye browed, pot-bellied husband within this grotesque vision standing before her. 'What have you done?' she whispers.

'I have found a job, guaranteed with regular pay. This is the uniform.' He raises the red-purple length of flimsy synthetic cloth again. A sob escapes her mouth.

'Woman! Help me wear this saree.' He booms.

Centuries old conditioning finds its mark. Sharmila takes the soft, grainy, gently unfolding length of fabric from her husband's hand, while tears form within the wells of her eyes. Rabin picks up the matching blouse, neatly ironed and folded on the bed, and inserts both his arms in the sleeves, as if wearing a button-down shirt.

The sleeves of the blouse stick to his forearms and the back rides up his back. He resembles a weightlifter with a heavy barbell on his back. He begins to wrestle with the blouse, twisting and turning, while his potbelly jiggles ferociously.

Happy laughter bursts forth from Sharmila. Laughing, and with tears streaming from her eyes, she retrieves her husband from the grip of the deadly blouse. He smiles tentatively at her, as she helps him put his arms in, one at a time, and buttons up. She frowns, and turns away to pick up the pressed petticoat. She spreads it out on the floor, and jerks her chin to indicate that he put his feet within the hole formed. When he does so, she slides the skirt up his pink-waxed legs, and ties it tightly around his waist.

Avoiding her husband's penetrating, pleading eyes, she tucks and pleats and pins up the saree around his frame. As she gets ready to pin the pallu, the end of the saree to his shoulder, he stops her with his palm. She looks up at him, hope filling her tear-stained eyes. He bends down to take a large roll of cotton and tears up two large swaths. He forms them into large balls, and stuffs them into the drooping cups of the blouse, filling them up and adjusting them. Her neatly pleated pallu unfolds from her hands and swishes over the floor, as Sharmila watches her husband's bust size grow larger than her own.

Wracking sobs fill her body. She drops the safety pin and rushes out of their room. Rabin watches his wife run away, from him. He looks into the mirror. 'Is this saree clad, large breasted figure, Rabin Roy? Maybe, maybe not. Maybe it is Robin Roy. Yes, she is not running away from me. Sharmila is running away from this hideous Robin Roy, with large breasts and metallic lips.' Robin stares into the mirror, materialising herself into existence. Her lips tremble, her eyes dart, her eyebrows arch, her hands flutter.

At last, as she hums an item-song, she glues the braided bun wig on her head, pins up the edge of the pallu to her shoulder, clasps the gem-studded, dangling bangles and earrings, picks up her matching turquoise hand-bag, and while swishing her waist side-to-side, swaggers out of the room.

The Siamese fighting fishes, free of the barrier dividing them, fight. The agitated water around them is a kaleidoscope of colours—ruby-red and livid purple.

The Man in the Shadows
PALO STICKLAND

Other children's mothers waited at the school gate, but Reetu didn't mind that she walked home alone because she knew it wasn't Ma's fault. Ma was ill. When Reetu's father died, her mother took to bed with a myriad of aches and pains brought on by grief and her diabetic condition. That's what she told everyone. Through school and college, Reetu would leave her friends early, to hurry home.

'Don't leave me,' her mother would sob. 'You're all I have left.'

Each morning and evening since Reetu's tenth birthday, her mother had made her light incense and offer prayers to Mother Kali, one of the seven sister goddesses.

She said, 'Your skin is as dark as Mata Kali's. She, of them all, will be sure to protect you. What a pity, you take after your father.'

This confused Reetu because she could see that her father was light-skinned. Her mother had persisted. She showed Reetu a photograph. A line of seven grown-ups stood in a veranda in India looking into the lens: at their feet sat a group of children, itching to move away and resume their games. It had been taken years ago, on a family visit to India. Those cousins lived in New York: she hadn't heard from them since. Her mother pointed behind the aunts,

46

uncles and Grandma, to a man who stood, out of focus in the shadows, leaning against the wall at the back.

'Your father,' she said.

Reetu didn't believe her. Papa was her father, and when he came home that evening he would help her with her homework. Ma was ill, and not thinking straight. Now, twenty years later, Reetu knew her mother was dying. Even the doctor, who had always been positive, had said it wouldn't be long. The nurses visited twice a day, looking solemn, making her mother comfortable.

When the end came, she knew. Her mother's body shivered, her face took on a grimace as if there was deep, excruciating pain inside. Reetu smoothed her hands over the dying woman's features, then took her pulse. It was very faint, fading away until there was nothing.

'Goodbye, Ma,' Reetu whispered. She stood with her hand on her mother's heart for a few minutes, looking down at the once beautiful face, then arranged the quilt thinking that everything should be presentable for those who would come into the room now.

She walked to the window, drew the pink, rose-patterned curtains and stood looking out on the beautiful summer's day. The street, with its suburban, detached villas surrounded by neatly-tended gardens, space for vehicles at the side, lived on, oblivious to her mother's passing. Touching the curtains, she remembered how her mother had loved pretty things. The clink of glass bangles, the sparkle of gemstones on her rings, the smooth sheen of gold around her neck; those were the sights and sounds of Tara Singh, who was no more. Reetu hated all the pretty things.

She reached for the phone to call the surgery before taking the bangles from her mother's wrists, then the chain from around her neck and finally the hoop earrings she'd always worn. She placed them in the jewellery box. From the top of the chest of drawers she lifted the jug of water with its matching tumbler and carried them downstairs to the kitchen.

After that, Reetu was too busy talking to the nurse, the doctor and the funeral assistants to think of grieving but when they placed the plastic body bag beside her mother she backed away, grabbing the curtain for support.

The young woman noticed and said, 'Would you like more time, Reetu?'

'No. I'm fine, really. Go ahead.' Reetu nodded, swallowed, her hands sweaty.

When the zip was closed over her mother's face, Reetu turned away. The young male assistant, tall and thin, with a serious pale face which was perfect for the job that he did, paused, looking towards her, waiting.

There was an awkward silence, then Reetu took a deep breath, 'Shall I walk in front? To open the door for you?'

'Yes, please.' He held out a file.

'This is for you to read, and bring to the office. We'll see you later, then?'

Reetu nodded. They lifted her mother's body onto a stretcher, and she led the way downstairs to the front door.

She watched them walk, with ease, down the flower-lined path. Her mother was so light now, Reetu had been able to lift her into the bath by herself.

No more of these guilt feelings, she admonished herself. I've done a lifetime of caring. However, as the stretcher was slid into a van marked 'Private Ambulance' and the doors slammed shut, she leaned on the door and felt the tears course down her cheeks.

Three weeks later, she'd lived through the funeral, listened to her relatives commiserations, some heartfelt, others entirely false, and felt a huge sense of relief. She booked a flight to Delhi. She stood at the living room window waiting for the taxi to Glasgow Airport thinking, I've lost all my friends, but once this is done, I'll work on a new life. Ma thought there was something in India for me. Reetu remembered each day sitting at her mother's side, as she drifted in and out of consciousness, whispering, calling and repeating names and incidents.

'Ram is waiting.' That, Reetu thought she understood. Her father was called Ram, he's waiting in heaven for her mother. Fine.

'Oh Reetu, your sister, Baby, is leaving.'

'I've lost my boy. Help me, Reetu!'

'You must go to India. Find the mound. Three fields along from the canal. You can do it.'

Reetu turned these ramblings over in her mind, but couldn't make sense of them. Neither of her parents had ever mentioned a sister, or a brother. There were no photos, no papers. Once her mother woke looking so happy to see her, called her Baby, but on realising it was Reetu, looked disappointed.

Reetu tried to laugh it off. 'Who did you think I was, Ma?' But it was too late. Her mother turned away, leaving Reetu wondering about Baby. She asked, but her mother refused to answer.

On arrival in Delhi, Reetu became busy with disembarkation procedures. Then, finding her way to the railway station required all her concentration, but as soon as she was on the train, it hit her that she was in the most colourful of places. And here, people were as dark as she was which made her feel good, the same as everyone, except when she turned around at the ticket booth.

'May God grant you a son.' The woman held out her hand for alms, and gestured to the sickly child on her hip.

Reetu had shrunk away. Now, safe in the air-conditioned first class carriage, she felt foolish and ashamed. This is India, she thought, life is hard here, not like my soft middle-class Scottish home.

She watched the sad tiny slum houses slip along the railway track in Delhi. Then it was green fields and the new roads being built. She wondered at the lives of the women labourers lifting rubble as the train sped past them towards the north. At last, she alighted at her destination.

Out in the dusty bustling street, she hired a taxi, telling the driver, 'I wish to go to Navpind.'

Twenty minutes later on the outskirts of the village, he asked her, 'To what family do you belong?'

She replied, 'My grandfather's name is Hari Singh.'

The driver stopped for directions from a group of old men who sat under a huge, ancient banyan tree. A few minutes later he stopped and Reetu recognised the old iron gate from her mother's photos. Paying the driver she stepped out, rolled her case to the entrance door in the gate and lifted the heavy latch. She entered a large, u-shaped courtyard with trees down the middle. A deep veranda shaded each room, of which there were six along each side of the u and four at the back. She walked towards the corner room on the right for she knew, again from photographs, the door would lead to her parents' sitting room with the dining room and kitchen leading off from it. In the opposite corner of the house an old woman, dressed in black with a white scarf, sat in a rocking chair. Reetu wondered if she should greet her first, but the woman's eyes were closed. Taking her mother's keys from her backpack, Reetu matched their numbers to those on the padlock hanging from the latch on the green door. The second key fitted the lock and she pushed into the room. Inside, there was a bed, a large steel trunk and a steel wardrobe. An archway led to another room to her right where she could make out a table and chairs. Everything including the floor, was covered with a thick layer of dust. Reetu lifted her scarf to her mouth to prevent herself coughing, and stepped backwards out of the room. She turned, walking with firm steps to the rocking chair. The woman rose just as Reetu reached her. The surprisingly light grey, wide-awake eyes held a confident, appraising gaze. Reetu smiled.

'Praise to the Mother Goddess,' was the woman's greeting.

'Namaste. I'm Reetu, Ram Singh's daughter. My mother, Tara...' Reetu began.

'I know who you are. You couldn't be anyone else. Your mother. Tara. She locked her rooms. That's why you are greeted by dust. I am Durgi. Your uncle left me to care for the house, to clean the unlocked rooms. So, you are here because Tara is dead now?'

'Yes. A month ago.'

Durgi nodded, 'You are welcome, bring your case to this room,' the old woman pointed behind her. 'I am paid to keep it clean for anyone returning from foreign parts.'

Reetu thanked her, turning to roll her case to the room where there was a large bed and a sideboard full of photographs. She was lifting each photo to the light when Durgi spoke behind her. 'See, these are your cousins. A beautiful family. You know them, yes?'

'No. We live in Glasgow, the others are in America. I met them when I was little, but I don't remember much about them. Yes, they are beautiful. I would like to meet them.'

'It will not be possible because they are all dead. Except for Bobby, who is in a wheelchair. Why is it that you are dark, but they were all so fair?' Durgi raised her eyebrows, giving an almost mocking smile.

Reetu felt sorry for this old servant whose favourite family were dead. She shrugged, 'How awful that they're all gone. I didn't know. Does it matter, I mean, about colour?'

Durgi looked away, saying sternly, 'You should use that cupboard for your clothes. I will give you the keys. Lock everything; it is better for everyone. I will cook food now.'

'Oh. Thank you.' Reetu replaced a photo and turned towards Durgi, but she had gone to the kitchen. She found the photograph where she was sitting with her cousins in front of the adults. There was the man in the shadows. What had her mother said about him, so long ago?

During the next two days, Reetu emptied her mother's trunk and wardrobe, to air the contents, but there were no clues to a lost boy or a baby. She asked Durgi the way to the canal and walked there, passing three fields on either side, but there was no mound.

That night she questioned the old woman, 'Why is the canal dry? I thought it would be taking water to the fields.'

'Nowadays, most farmers use electric tube-wells to bring the water from deep below the fields. The canal is not used unless the dam, high in the hills, is overflowing. Then water is released and the canal becomes a playground.'

'What fun! I was looking for a mound, a little hill?' Reetu could see amusement grow in Durgi's eyes.

'Did Tara tell you about her little trysts at the mound? No?' Reetu had looked surprised, and saw in the old face, the enjoyment of disclosing a juicy secret. 'She did not say where you were conceived? We all knew her husband could not give her babies. That is why she met her lover at the mound, and prayed for children at the shrine. The mound was cleared and now it is only flat land. Why do you ask?' Again, Durgi gave that knowing, mocking look.

Reetu was quiet for many minutes. Papa is not my father? I was conceived in the fields? That's why Ma kept rambling on about the mound?

She couldn't hold back the retort, 'You already know, Durgi. You know everything, don't you?

'You have been alone too long, my child,' the older woman said fastening her grey eyes firmly on Reetu's brown ones. 'Do not dig up the past.'

Reetu began to pace up and down the veranda. 'Did I have a brother and a sister? My mother said there was a lost boy and a girl who went away.'

'She should have told you herself. Always a selfish woman.' Durgi clicked her tongue.

'Ma was ill.'

'Hiding behind illness because she felt guilty, knowing it was her fault the boy was lost. Her fault she could only look after one child and sent the other away.'

'It's true? Are they alive? My father, brother and sister?'

'I do not know. This problem is too big for you, child. Too many bad deeds and evil thoughts are in the past. You are better to leave it. Go back to your home.'

'I am alone in Scotland. If there's any chance of them being alive, I have to try to find them.' Reetu continued pacing the courtyard, throwing pleading glances at the old woman.

Finally, Durgi nodded, 'Right. You must call to Mother Goddess. Remember, it is not done lightly. If she gives you help, then I am with her. If she is against you, you may not survive. The calling is serious.'

'Goddess Kali? My mother insisted I pray to her. I'm not afraid. What do I do?'

'In two days, it will be the new moon. You must be in the fields, at the shrine of the old mound. Everyone knows it is a place of great power.'

They made preparations. 'You will bathe and wear black, all new clothes; and take black urid dahl, the symbol of darkness and of black magic. Green cardamom and cloves, symbols of female and male power and molasses - to sweeten the Goddess.' Durgi smiled.

On the appointed night, in the darkness before the rising of the new moon, at the shrine which was a tiny white temple near where the mound had been, Reetu stripped off all her clothes. She arranged the symbols of male and female power at her feet, and threw the pulses over her head. Then, she took two lumps of molasses in each hand, raised her arms and called out, 'Mother Goddess Kali, give me strength! Help me find my people! I call you seven times!'

At the seventh call, a wind swirled around Reetu, until she felt lifted into the air and spun around. Then, she was let down as the wind rushed upwards to the moon, now clearly visible. Reetu felt herself grow weak and fall. She was caught and covered with a sheet. Durgi placed her arms around the young woman's shoulders and took her home to bed.

Reetu woke to find the old woman at her bedside, rocking gently in her chair. 'What happened?' she asked.

'You slept for two days. It is good.'

'Did it work? What we did?'

'We wait. You rest and be strong.'

Next day, Reetu was having breakfast in her mother's room, and watching through the window as Durgi rocked in her chair in the veranda. The cleaner came to whisper into the old woman's ear, and place a chair beside her. Durgi smiled.

Ten minutes later, a big man stepped through the door in the gate.

He paused to look around before shouting in an American accent, 'Durgi! What is the meaning of this?'

Reetu rose from the table. Her uncle, who else could it be? Light-skinned, short-haired, wearing an immaculately tailored suit of white summer-weight material, he stomped up to the old woman.

'Praise to the Mother Goddess,' said Durgi. 'It is Bobby! No wheelchair?'

'I woke up two days ago, and I walked. Then came the urge to return to India. What magic did you perform, you old trickster?'

He touched Durgi's feet, accepted her blessing and sat down on the chair.

'It was the grace of the Mother Goddess, Bobby, and she wishes you to meet your niece. Come, Reetu.' Durgi's hands beckoned to her, then began to make 'waves' in the air, almost unnoticed and unobtrusive.

Bobby gazed down at his knees, his ankles and then his toes which he wriggled in his sandals. Then he sighed and looked up at Reetu.

'Sorry we never met before, kid.'

'Uncle Bobby, Namaste.' Reetu stood with hands folded in greeting. 'Why was it that we didn't meet?'

'Well, life happened,' he shrugged as Durgi flashed a piercing glance at him which made him rise to greet his niece, opening his arms to her. 'It's just you and me, kid. All the family that's left.'

Bobby really did look sad, Reetu thought, as she moved into his all-enveloping embrace. At that moment, the gate creaked open and someone else came in, a thin dark elderly man who paused at the gate to look in at the three people under the veranda. They turned to look.

Bobby gave a yelp like a frightened puppy and raised his hands to his head.

'Durgi? Is that Ram Kumar?' he shouted. Durgi tightened her lips and continued waving her fingers. Reetu's mind worked at lightning speed. Ram, the same as Papa. Thank you, dear Goddess Kali, he is here. The man in the shadows. My father, that's what Ma said.

Behind Ram walked a young woman dressed in traditional salwar kameez, so different from Reetu's jeans and short top but there was no mistaking the resemblance between them. She was Reetu's twin.

The child who left. Baby.

As Baby walked towards her, tears welled up in Reetu's eyes. What a heartbreaking decision for Ma to make. To separate them.

Ram approached Durgi's rocking chair, leaned over and touched both her feet. She blessed him with the words, 'Live long.'

Bobby stretched to his full height, took a deep breath and said to Durgi, 'Is that all of us, then? Now, don't mention the goddess.'

But it was Reetu who spoke, 'Uncle Bobby, I called Goddess Kali. I needed her help because Ma told me to come back. Durgi helped me, and here we are. But, what about the boy who was lost?' She glanced at Durgi, who stared at Bobby, and continued waving her fingers.

There was silence, then Bobby cleared his throat and began, 'See here, it was a long time ago. I'm sure I was crazy. You know, Reetu, like you might say in England, mentally disturbed? Big time.' Taking a large, white handkerchief from his pocket, he blew his nose.

'In Scotland,' Reetu gave him an icy glare.

Bobby stood up. 'I know what you want, Durgi. Let's go.'

'I want the truth. Give me your arm, Bobby.' She let him help her up. They walked down the courtyard at Durgi's pace. Slow, small steps.

Reetu's twin took her hand, Ram blessed her, placing his hand on her head. They walked together, hand in hand, following Bobby and Durgi.

'Uncle Bobby, what happened to my cousins, the ones in the photos?'

'Life happened, kid. Son of a bitch old life. I was one of three brothers, Reetu. The other one had two kids. I had three, two girls and a boy. Accidents, illness, all gone in twenty-five years. We were cursed. Did you do it, Durgi?' He stared down at her.

Durgi seemed to be shushing a small person at her side, but Reetu couldn't see anyone.

'Not me, Bobby. Your grandmother, she did not take kindly to losing a grandson.'

At this point, Reetu was sure Durgi had looked up and smiled, as if seeing someone tall walking with her. Grandma? 'Uncle Bobby, is something strange happening?'

'Uh-huh. Yeah kid. You called them. They're all here. Aren't they, Durgi?'

'Of course. Keep walking, Bobby. How far now?'

Near the gate, Bobby stopped, took several deep breaths, rubbed his face with his handkerchief, and turned to his right. It was the entrance to the byre which at one time housed the family's four milk cows: the mangers still stood against the wall. At the back there was a newer patch of brick work. They gathered in front of it.

Bobby fell to his knees, blubbering, 'God knows, I've paid for it. I was insane with jealousy. I ordered the boy killed because he was your son Ram, and not mine. I loved Tara. Asked her to have my child, but she chose you, the untouchable cleaner...' Bobby's head touched the ground as he bawled, drumming the floor with his fists.

Ram, who once lifted the family's excrement in a tin bowl to take to the fields every morning, said nothing. He walked to the corner, took a pick-axe and began to demolish the wall. Durgi, Reetu, Baby-twin and Bobby watched. Inside the cupboard size space was a hessian bag tied at the neck, big enough for a three-year-old child. In it were several large stones.

Ram explained, 'I discovered your plan, paid your hired killer to bury stones and to give me the child.'

A chill breeze swept through the byre. Durgi had her truth.

'That means, I wasn't the cause of his death! I was cursed for nothing?' Bobby stood up.

'The boy lived.' Ram stretched up to look behind the group to the entrance of the byre. They turned, and saw a man, a younger Ram, a male version of the twins.

Reetu gasped. 'This is the lost boy? Ma never knew he'd survived.'

Ram, who was now smiling, moved to greet the boy. Durgi patted Bobby on the head and bid him rise off his knees, but the difference in Reetu was the most amazing. She had found her people. The three siblings hugged and left the building together, holding hands and chatting. Reetu, who hadn't laughed in years, now couldn't stop.

The Other Side of the Bridge
SERENA PATEL

25 September 2017

Dearest Aani,

It's been 49 days since I last saw you. Summer has become autumn. The leaves have started to turn from green to gold and there is a chill in the air that wasn't there when I last held you in the warmth of the summer sun.

I miss you every second of every day, I can't believe I can't be with you, hold your hand or kiss your lips. It's so difficult being apart.

Do you remember how we would sit in the park for hours, talking and talking, about so much and nothing at all. I would be telling you the story of Dad and the time he took us fishing in his sherwani and you'd laugh with that twinkle in your eye. I'd give anything to hear your laugh now, to see your beautiful eyes.

It seems so unfair that all this is out of our control, we voted against the border. I can't help but wonder how many families were torn apart when they split Scotland and England. How many lovers like us living in neighbouring towns are now divided by the great iron bridge?

They opened the gates today for deliveries and for a second I thought about sprinting across back to England, back to you.

There are military police all along the border, watching night and day. It seems unreal, like something out of a movie. Except it's not a movie and we have to live with the consequences of a decision we didn't make.

How are you? I miss you so much, I said that already didn't I but I do, I can't wait for us to be together again. It's killing me that we have to wait for an official piece of paper before you can come here and be my wife.

All my love
Amir.

4 October 2017

My wonderful Amir,

I miss you too. I dreamed of us last night, we were walking in the forest. The night sky was so clear, the moon and stars lit our path. I felt so calm and safe. Then I woke up and for a second it was as though none of this had happened. No referendum, no bridge, no border. Just for a second everything was okay again.

Then I remembered and all our dreams came crashing down around me.

Life here is difficult. There are groups of extremists who believe that now England is independent, anyone who is not white should leave. My little sister is being bullied at school, I guess the kids learn from their parents. It's frightening that people I thought I knew really well were the very same people who voted to cut us off from the rest of Europe. It's hard not to feel isolated. Racism seems accepted by so many now. How could we ever bring children into a world where they will be told they don't belong?

The visa application is taking a long time, so many forms and questions. I wish we had just married when we had the chance, I would be with you now.

Love Aani.

18 October 2017

My Beautiful Aani,

Are you okay? I heard there was rioting near your town. I pray you and your family are safe and well. Please let me know you are okay.

It is so difficult not being able to talk to you on the telephone, the networks are still down here, there is no sign of when we will have internet access either. There are rumours it is the governments way of controlling everything, I don't know if that's true but it feels like we are blind without a real view or access to the outside world.

I think my family are secretly glad we are apart, they were never completely happy with not being able to arrange a marriage for me. I think they were just humouring me to be honest. I want to hate them for it but they are all I have here.

My father says I should forget you, we live in different worlds now but I cannot. I will not. How can it be that you are so close yet I cannot reach you?

The moment you get here we will get our wedding arranged. If you will still have me.

Amir.

25 October 2017

Aani,

It has been a week since my last letter and I have heard nothing from you. Please let me know you are okay.

The news bulletin gives very little information but at work one of the doctors told me that the riots are destroying whole towns in England. People seem to have lost their minds. My Muslim friend, Rukhsana said her aunts shop in Newcastle was broken into and the looters painted 'Go home Pakis' on the front window. England seems so broken now, I feel frightened for our future. I wish you were here with me.

Please let me know you are safe.

Amir

25 October 2017

Darling Amir,

I'm so sorry I couldn't write to you sooner. We had to leave our house and go to Aunty Meena's place in the next town so if you have written to me I haven't received it. Our street was set alight by the rioters, some families didn't get away, the screams were horrific, I can't sleep at night now, I'm so afraid.

I have written Aunty Meena's address on the back of the envelope, I think we will be here for now.

Papa says if we can be married soon I can bring the family with me to Scotland and everyone will be safe again.

I try to make sense of it all but can't. It seems only the other day that England and Scotland were all part of the UK. Then so much terrorism and death in the world, so much anger and blame. The European referendum changed everything and suddenly Scotland wanted to break away and the English are so angry with everyone who looks different to them. The world is so different now Amir. I know not all people are hateful but it seems the extremists have a voice and perhaps they are right, perhaps we don't belong here anymore, part of me fears we never did.

I find myself thinking about Punjab even though I've only been there once before, when I was a child. I remember being surprised at the way they lived over there. My grandmother would wash the clothes outside in the river with a bar of soap. I couldn't understand why they didn't have a washing machine. The farm our family lives on over there is so far removed from how we grew up. I didn't feel like I belonged there though, I was so different to everyone else. I found the hard dusty ground difficult to walk on where everyone else walked barefoot with ease. My Punjabi was terrible, my grandmother moaned at Papa for not teaching me properly. My clothes were all pretty new and my cousins relied on hand me downs. But they seemed happy, I guess they didn't know any different. Even the food was different, at home we had so much choice and sometimes still we are not content, in India they survive on so little and yet they don't complain. I felt guilty and discontent all at the same time. Papa said I was a sulky ungrateful child and he would leave me there to learn a good lesson. I cried and cried for a whole afternoon.

I don't know why I'm thinking of Punjab, I didn't belong there and maybe I don't belong here, where is home now Amir? Will it ever be okay?

22 November 2017

Dear Aani,

Why don't you reply, I have sent four letters now and no reply. I heard through a friend at the hospital that rioters set some houses alight in your town. I pray you were not hurt but I hear nothing from you and my hope dies a little each day.

Please send me word that you are okay.

Amir

27 November 2017

My darling Amir,
You didn't reply to my last letter, is everything okay?

We are still at Aunty Meena's house, it's a bit cramped with all of us sharing a two bedroom house but at least we are safe for now.

The visa office contacted me, I have an interview with the immigration officer next week. I'm worried they'll reject my application Amir, what if I can't get to you?

Please reply soon so that I know you're okay.

Aani

1 December 2017

My Dearest Aani,

I am sending this with little hope that you will ever read it. I have to accept you are gone. The news showed burning buildings in your town and other northern cities in England. The rioting seems to have taken over normal life there and people are dying. I wish I had done more to save you, I should have done more.

I love you Aani, I always will.

My father says its time to move on, I can't face life without you but I'm the eldest and they expect me to carry on the family name. They want me to meet a girl from a family they have known for years. What do I do Aani? How can I be with anyone else but you?

I'm so sorry Aani, I'm so so sorry.

Amir.

17 December 2017

Amir,

You haven't replied to my letters, has the post been getting through? It doesn't matter because I'm coming. The immigration officer approved my application! I told her our story and because I also have a job offer at the hospital there I have enough points to qualify. This time next week I will be in your arms and we can plan our future Amir. How amazing will that be!

My family are sad that I am leaving but they know I will be safe with you and once we are married they can join us. I have so much hope now Amir. I can't wait to see you.

All my love,

Aani

5 January 2018

Amir,

You didn't see me yesterday, but I saw you. My heart is broken. How could you?

I could smell the sweet scent of ladoo mixed with fragrant spices on the breeze as I walked down your street with such anticipation and excitement. I thought to myself someone must be getting married, how lovely.

I stopped around the corner from your street to check my appearance in a car window. I wanted to be perfect for you, for your family. I was nervous, it had been so long, would you still love me the same? All the difficulties we had been through getting your family to accept us as a couple, all the pain of being apart but it was worth it. We were going to be together now. We belong together.

Music filled my ears as I walked down your street and my spirits soared to hear the sounds of our childhood.

Then I saw it. The cerise ribbon adorning the white rolls Royce, gleaming in the winter sunlight. I saw the flower garlands draped along the front of your house and I heard the sound of aunties and grandmothers singing songs older than time.

Not just any wedding. Your wedding.

They were leading you out of the house, you looked so handsome in your sherwani and the look of pride on your mothers face just shattered me. I felt dizzy but I couldn't let anyone see me so I crouched down behind a car, watching furtively from a distance. Tears streamed down my face but my voice was lost. This can't be happening I kept telling myself.

When the wedding car left and the people had dispersed I stood not knowing where to go. I made this move for you, to be with you. Now what? How could you betray me like that, why would you do this? A thousand questions whirling round in my mind.

I looked up and saw your father standing outside the house, he was getting ready to get in his car and join you at the temple I suppose. He spotted me and stared for what felt like forever. I felt frozen in time. I thought he might speak but instead he got into the car and drove away.

Humiliated and in shock I sat on the steps opposite your house for a long time. The winter sunset bathed the street in a warm orange glow but I sat shivering. Eventually I got up to leave. I didn't want to be there when you returned with your new bride.

I walked a little looking at the streets we had walked through together so many times. The memories of us hurt too much so I started running, no direction, no sense of where I should go now, escape was my only thought.

Eventually I stopped, it was late and there were very few people around. I thought of what you would be doing now.

Making a speech to your loved ones, dancing with your bride?

I should have made my way to the bus station and gone back to the bridge but I didn't, couldn't.

I am staying in a B&B in town, I don't know what to do now. Should I go home to a country where I no longer feel welcome? I can't stay, I don't belong here either.

I wish I knew why.

Aani.

14 February 2018

Oh Aani,

How can you ever forgive me. I thought you were dead. I am writing this with no knowledge of where to send it. How do I reach you?

I found a pile of your letters, my father had been hiding them from me. I'm devastated that you were so close to me on the day I got married. Had I known I would have stopped it all.

I confronted my father but he actually defended what he had done saying it was for the best. I told him I would leave my wife, get a divorce. He said the family would disown me, I would be an outcast.

I couldn't believe my ears, I stormed out and now I'm sitting in the freezing cold in the park writing this without an address to send it to.

I realised it is Valentine's Day today, it had totally slipped my mind. I remember it was always a special time for us, it's just too painful without you.

I got married Aani, they pushed me into it but I thought you were dead. No-one could ever replace you, no-one.

I wish I knew where you are, you are the one I want, not this woman who is my wife. I barely know her. Since the wedding I try desperately not to be alone with her. There are expectations, comments about grandchildren from my mother.

I wish I had known the truth before I made this commitment. I wish I knew where you are.

We heard through a relative that your father died of a heart attack, your mother is very unwell now too. Where are you Aani, your family needs you.

I hope you are safe and well, I know I hurt you terribly. Words can never make up for that.

We don't get to choose where the lines of love are drawn Aani but there are some boundaries we cannot cross. Marriage feels like a cage, I don't know if I can get out.

Amir.

14 February 2019

Dearest Amir,

I will never post this letter but I felt I had to write it. I saw you today as I do most Sunday mornings in the park with your family. You never notice me, I am the figure sitting on the bench, hood and collars up to protect my face from recognition as well as the cold winter air. You looked happier than you have in a long time, at peace. It hurt but I was glad for you. Your wife is beautiful, she looks at you with love in her eyes and that hurts too. You were dressed in your winter boots, waterproof coats and jeans, you looked like something out of a catalogue strolling through the park without a care in the world. Little giggles floated across the park and you leaned over into the buggy and lifted her out. Your little girl. The most precious little girl in the world because she's yours. The park melted away and it was me walking with you and it was our baby. Except it wasn't and that dream will never be mine now.

Seeing you today made me realise I am living my life through you still. I'm moving further north to the coast. Perhaps I can find myself there. I don't seem to be here or anywhere else anymore. A big part of me doesn't want to leave, would prefer to stay sitting on the bench waiting for you. I have to say goodbye Amir, I will never forget you. It's time for me to find some kind of happiness even if it's not the life I planned.

Aani.

A Safe Place

FARAH AHAMED

Langata Prison, Nairobi, December 2008

Kay slept on a thin mattress with a torn blanket to cover her. In the corner of her cell was a steel bucket and a brown sponge for wiping both her body and the rough walls finished with gloss grey. The bulb hanging from the corrugated iron roof was never turned on. The only light coming in was through the barbed wire in the narrow ventilation gap between the roof and walls. Her cell, at the end of a long, wide corridor, had a small internal window with bars which overlooked the passageway lined with other cells on either side. These were shared by five or six women. Once a day, before they were marched out to the fields, they ate together in the passage seated on low stools. Kay slept and ate on her own.

'Oi,' she shouted. 'There's a cockroach in here.'

'What is it this time, Mchawi?' the warden said, standing outside the door of Kay's cell.

'My name's not Mchawi, you know that.'

'We can call you what we like, witch. In here you're Mchawi.'

The warden pushed a Bible between the bars. 'Read this.'

'Vermin are everywhere. Don't you see them?' Kay said. 'Even God can't help.'

'What are you talking about? Jesus forgives everyone, even sinners like you.'

'I'm not a sinner. I'm the same as you.'

'You're a witch, internally displaced.' The warden adjusted the brass buckle on her green and brown trousers and rolled up the sleeves of her khaki sweater. 'We are not the same.'

'I keep telling you, I'm not a witch.'

'I know what I've been told, and why you're in solitary confinement. And if you know what's good for you, you'll shut up. Here are your supplies.'

Six boiled sweets, a box of Nice biscuits and a packet of sanitary towels landed on the cell floor.

'Look at this,' Kay said picking up the pads. 'Clin & Cleer. Made in China. Fully absorbent. We need Clean and Clear in Kenya.'

'Mchawi don't be smart with me.'

Through the small barred window she could see in the corner of the corridor, a black and white television encased in a steel cage suspended from the roof.

'Can you turn that blasted screen this way?' she shouted. 'I want to know what's going on outside.'

'Wewe, Mchawi, nyamaza,' the warden said. 'Keep quiet and read the Bible. This isn't your husband's house.'

#

It had started on her last birthday. She didn't know how long ago that was. She and El were living in the UK then,

76

and they'd arranged a special dinner together, but at the last minute he'd called to say he had an urgent meeting. Kay spent the evening on her own and when El returned, he told her he must go back to Kenya to organise some important projects. He asked her to go with him. After their return home, she'd been preoccupied with settling down in their new house and starting work at the school close by and it had taken her awhile to notice that El was always in his study with the door shut. She'd asked him what the big secret was, and he always replied, 'Is that coffee I smell?' He would hug her and she would forget to pursue her question.

#

Hearing the clanging of gates in the corridor, Kay got up from the mattress and went to the window. A shaft of sunlight fell across the floor. Two dozen women in blue and white uniforms like her own, trudged past, back from their planting.

'Hello,' she shouted. She picked up one of the sweets and flung it through the bars. It hit one of the women, who turned and snapped.

'You bitch, Mchawi? What's your problem?'

Kay picked up the Bible and hurled it through the window, just missing the woman's shoulder. Five women gathered around the door.

'Mchawi, nobody loves you,' one said.

'Not true,' she said. 'My husband loves me. He's coming to take me home tomorrow.'

'He doesn't love you,' the woman taunted. 'If he did, he wouldn't have brought you here.'

The warden appeared. 'What's going on?' She picked up the Bible. 'Mchawi is a curse on everyone. Outside and in here.' She tapped the woman on the shoulder with her baton. 'Get back into your cell,' she ordered. 'Who do you talk to all the time, Mchawi, walking up and down and waving your hands like this and like that?'

'Right now I'm talking to you,' she said. 'And when you're not here, I talk to my children. Do you have children?'

'I do, but what's it to you?'

'I did too. See, I'm just like you.'

The inmates were still in the corridor staring at Kay.

'What are you gawping at?' she shouted.

'Get back to your cells,' the warden said. 'I've told you before, no one's allowed to talk to Mchawi.'

She lay down on the mattress and hugged her blanket against the cold and damp. She shut her eyes blocking out the grey. What did these stupid women understand about love? She turned onto her side. El had promised to come and see her and bring whatever she needed. She stared at the cement floor, its crevices filled with crumbs of rotting food and filth. A cockroach almost the size of her forefinger darted out of the corner and stopped at the edge of the mattress, near her feet, its feelers moving up and down. She watched as it advanced slowly on to the mattress and up the blanket towards her arm, stopping by her wrist. She opened her palm. The insect climbed on to her hand and ran up her left arm. She brought her right palm down sharply, but the roach jumped onto the blanket and scuttled off. She chased after it, but there was no trace. She shook the blanket and lay down again.

#

That morning they'd been late for school. When they reached the gates, Kay saw billows of black smoke surrounding the main academic block. She shouted to El to phone for help. Dozens of villagers gathered around with buckets of water. From the building came the screams of children. An hour went by and no one came to the rescue.

'Who could have done such a thing?' she asked, later. 'And to the children?' 'Don't ask too many questions,' El said.

'I'll ask until I get answers.'

'Your stubbornness will cost us.'

'I don't know what you mean.'

'This is about my loyalty to The Party. They are my people. They have looked after me, paid for my education abroad, gave me money and now I have a place in the new government. I owe them. Try and understand.'

'It's you who must understand, El,' she said. 'You belong to me and I belong with you.'

'Stop right there Kay,' he said. 'I've heard enough of your childish, romantic nonsense.'

And after that he refused to speak to her until the following morning when he said, 'Kay, it's been decided it's not safe for you here anymore. It's best you go away, best for the campaign, best for us, for everyone.'

#

Kay kicked off the blanket and propped herself on her elbow. She scratched her arm, then her head and peered at the cracks in the floor. El said his friends would take her to a safe place. There'd been a mistake. He didn't know where she was, that's why he hadn't come to see her. She gazed at the gaps and fractures. Where was the damn thing hiding?

The silence was broken by shouting in the corridor. She got up and looked through the window. The inmates were arguing in different languages. The Luos didn't want to use the same wash buckets as the Kikuyus or Kalenjins, and the Kikuyus refused to sleep in the same cell as anyone from a different tribe.

'Who wants to share with me?' she shouted. 'I don't mind.'

'Shut up, you witch,' the warden intervened. 'No one was talking to you.' She threatened to lock the women together for a week with no planting, no extra-curricular activities, no gifts and no visitors. They swore as they were herded into their cells.

'What's your problem, Mchawi?' the warden said, coming over to Kay's door. 'Why do you incite the women?'

'Look how my scalp flakes and my skin itches. See how dry it is.' Kay scratched the word BASTARD on her arm with her nails. 'I need body lotion, I can't meet my husband like this. He loves my soft skin.'

The warden opened the door and placed a plate on the floor.

'I'm not hungry,' she said.

'Shut up and eat, I don't want problems from you.' The warden locked the door behind her and stayed by the window.

Kay sat on the mattress with the plate on her lap. She crumbled the usual white mound of ugali in her fingers. She tasted a clump, choked on the unsalted, powdery chunk and spat it out. Taking some more, she rolled it into a ball and placed it on the floor. She repeated this until she'd finished all the dough. Then she arranged the balls in a circle putting the sukuma between them. Wiping her hands on her uniform, she surveyed her design. White ball, green leaf, white ball, green leaf. El loved ugali, she'd make it for him every week and after dinner, they'd talk until the early hours of the morning, eating mandazi's and drinking tea. Every day at noon, he'd phone her.

'My coffee reminds me of you, Kay.'

'Why?' she'd ask, knowing the answer.

'It's strong, dark and sweet.'

What did El think of now when he smelt coffee? Of course he missed her. Tomorrow she'd go home and everything would be all right. She picked up the balls and crushed them. Then scooping up the crumbs, she scattered them around the room. He'd been looking for her all this time, and now at last he'd found her and was coming to take her home. She went on her knees, inspected a crack and filled it with scraps of ugali.

She lay on the mattress and gazed up at the bulb.

The next morning, Kay folded the blanket and shook out the mattress. As she arranged them in the corner, something black scurried out and disappeared again. She knelt and examined the fissures.

There was a rap on the door. 'Wewe, Mchawi, what are you looking for?'

She got up. 'Vermin.'

The warden threw in four pairs of knickers; red nylon, white cotton, frilly pink and black lace. 'Because your husband is coming,' she said. 'The NGO brought them yesterday.'

She held a pair to her waist and stretched them. 'But they're too small. I wear large.'

'Be grateful for what you get, Mchawi.'

She raised the knickers to her face, rubbing them against her nose and cheeks. Two inmates were watching at the window.

'Mchawi, what are you doing?' one said.

She waved the knickers. 'My husband's coming today. I'm going home.'

'Which ones will you wear?'

She lifted her uniform and without taking her eyes off the women, put on the red pair, then the black, then the white. 'Look,' she said. 'I'm wearing the colours of our flag.'

The women giggled. 'You're missing green.'

'Take these and give me green,' Kay said, throwing the pink knickers at the window. A skinny hand shot through the bars and caught them.

'You're Mchawi,' one woman said. 'You weren't loyal to your husband or your country; you don't deserve to wear our flag.'

'I was,' she said. 'And I do. I'm just like you.'

The women stared and turned away.

She sat on the floor. The tight elastic of the knickers bit into her skin, around her upper thighs and waist. She pulled off the white pair and then the red. El liked black lace.

She lay down on the mattress and tucked the knickers under her cheek, humming By the Rivers of Babylon. El loved Boney M. He'd grab a wooden spoon from the kitchen drawer and use it as a mic. Together, they'd sing their guts out, 'Now how shall we sing the Lord's song, in a strange land? Yeah, yeah, yeah.'

Tears fell onto the silky fabric. 'Ye-ah, we wept.'

The warden unlocked the door. 'Your visitor, your Bwana is here. Dadika kumi, ten minutes and no more.' She stepped aside and El entered.

'Hello Kay.' He looked around the cell, adjusted his tie and put his hands in his pockets. His cheeks were chubbier and a paunch showed under the grey pinstriped suit. A hint of familiar aftershave filled the stale air.

Kay got up. 'How kind of you to find the time to come and see me.'

He held out a white box. 'These are for you.'

Kay grabbed it and flung it at the wall. 'Where the hell have you been?'

'Wewe, Mchawi,' the warden shouted through the window. 'Chunga. Don't make trouble.'

'You shut up, this is my husband and I'll say what I like to him.' She turned to El. 'I've been waiting six fucking months.'

He took a tissue from his pocket and wiped his forehead. 'Kay, I can explain.'

'You said you were sending me to a safe place.'

'I didn't have a choice.'

'Why did they bring me here?'

'Try to understand. It's not so simple.'

'Why did they burn my school down? And what about my students?'

'Your memory is confused, I've explained it all before.'

She clutched at his lapels. 'Explain it to me again, at home.'

He took her hands, pushed her back gently and smoothed down his jacket. 'Your problem Kay, is you've never understood. If you had, we wouldn't be in this mess. The Party saw you as a threat with all your questions, and said you're not our kabila. I couldn't risk losing their trust.'

'So, this is your idea of a safe place?' She went over to the window and gripped the bars. 'Let us out,' she yelled. 'We're going home.'

The warden rapped on the door with her baton. 'Do you need help, Mzee?'

'Yes,' Kay said. 'Open the door.' She turned to El. 'Tell her to let us out.'

El wiped his forehead with his sleeve. 'Kay, try to understand.'

'What's going on?' She seized his jacket and shook him. 'I understand everything. Just take me home.'

'You don't get it, do you Kay?'

'What?'

'It's not safe for you out there.'

'What do you mean?'

'I owe them. The Party.'

'What are you talking about? I don't care about The Party. Just get me out of here.'

'I can't allow it; you're not one of us.'

She fell on her knees and grabbed his leg. 'I'm your wife.'

He staggered back. 'Let go of me.'

She clutched his trousers. 'Take me home.'

The warden knocked on the bars. 'Saa ame fika. Time's up.' She opened the door, pulled Kay away from El and slapped her face. 'Oi, Mchawi! Leave him alone.'

'Don't touch me.' Kay rubbed her cheek. 'You're a jerk El. Why are you here, then?'

He took a brown envelope from his jacket. 'I need you to sign these.'

'What are they?'

'Our divorce would prove my total allegiance to The Party.' He held out a pen. 'I have to stick with their agenda.'

She opened the cover and took out the papers. 'I deserted you, did I?' she said, slowly, turning the pages.

'You did Kay. You weren't loyal to The Party.'

'You abandoned me.'

'There's no point in arguing.'

She moved nearer to him and looked directly into his eyes. 'So you need my help now, do you?' She brought her face very close to his and smelt his aftershave and sweat. 'Why should I sign?'

He jerked his head back. 'You've damaged The Party enough. It's the least you could do.'

She waved the papers in his face. 'Get me out of here and I'll sign.'

'The Party order is clear. It must be a clean break.'

'You hear that?' Kay yelled to the warden. 'Clean and clear in Kenya.' She tore up the papers and threw them at him.

'I'll be back until you give in.'

'Get out.' She began to laugh. 'I'll never sign.'

'We'll see.' He bent to pick up the papers. 'The Party comes first.'

'Fuck The Party.'

El took a wad of notes from his pocket and gave them to the warden. 'Give her shampoo, soap and a towel; it smells like a sick dog in here.'

'You're the sick dog,' Kay said.

'Think about the papers,' he said.

The warden thumbed the notes. 'She was complaining her skin is too dry.'

'And no visitors,' El said. 'She's unstable and we don't want to upset her.'

'Sawa, sawa. No visitors. No problem.' The warden put the money in her pocket. 'She walks up and down, singing and talking to herself. Sometimes she sleeps. But she doesn't eat. She likes to be alone; ni Mchawi.'

El walked towards the door. 'Poor Kay,' he said, 'you've always had issues.'

'Mchawi,' the warden said. 'Do you hear that? Even your husband says you have issues.' She tucked her baton under her arm. 'You see how she refuses to cooperate, Mzee. Anya kataa kila kitu. And she provokes the other inmates. She's a witch.'

'Usi jali,' El said. 'Don't worry, she's safe in here.' He turned to Kay. 'Bye Kay, try and be good.' The warden escorted him out and locked the door.

Kay picked up the red and white knickers and hurled them at the door. 'I'll never sign,' she shouted. She sank to the floor and scratched BASTARD into her arm until it bled.

Several hours later, hearing music, Kay got up and went to the window. The warden was rounding up the inmates.

'The children are here,' she said. 'Remember, no fighting. Let's try and have a peaceful Christmas party.'

'Can I come?' Kay said.

'You don't qualify. This is for women in here, who have children out there. The kids have come to visit. You don't have children, Mchawi.'

'Those students were my children.'

'Read your Bible, maybe the Lord will inspire you today.' The warden marched the women in a single file towards the exit and pushed open the door, letting the sunlight fall across the floor. They trooped out and the warden locked the door. All was quiet and dark.

Kay sat down on the mattress and flipped through the Bible without reading, then began to tear out each page, one by one. She shredded the leaves into small pieces and arranged them in a mound, singing softly.

'Now how shall we sing the Lord's song in a strange place?' She blew on the pile sending the bits of paper scattering. She stared at the litter and large cracks in the floor, listening to the sound of children cheering in the distance. Then she went down on her hands and knees and began to scrape the filth out of each crack with her nails, peering into the crevices. The white box from El was on the floor by the door, and she ripped it open. Inside were twelve triangular doughnuts, mandazis, her favourite. She laughed as she arranged them in a circle around her.

'Brown girl in the ring tra la la la, la,' she sang, rocking herself. 'She looks like a sugar in a plum, plum, plum.'

She sat waiting.

Eurovision
NAMITA ELIZABETH CHAKRABARTY

For a long time in the English city known for its ivory towers she felt constantly in the midst of dinner parties, but without an invitation. When she went shopping for provisions there were people carefully choosing fine wines, reading labels and comparing prices, then adding in last minute purchases of cartons of olives or boxes of chocolates on the way to the till. On the way home, after a long day working, she would stare down from the upper deck of the bus, and through the window see people walking briskly along the pavement, tissue-wrapped bottles and bunches of flowers secured in their arms, while their hands held their phones, Google maps leading the way to addresses on invitations.

Despite the surface warmth of the picture postcard surroundings, honey-coloured stone houses and ancient buildings, there was something about her proximity but separation from the dinner parties that made her connect them in her mind with the shadows of the city. From the train, when she had travelled towards the city, she had glimpsed the outlines of military establishments hidden among the beautiful soft green hills and ancient dark green woodlands. And on the city buses she would often see khaki uniformed bodies, with muscular tall torsos, squashed between other bodies staring ahead, without eye contact. Generally though, either when waiting with their kitbags slung over their shoulders at the railway station, or more traditionally parading along the street in groups, the soldiers were seldom alone – unlike her.

There had been one family funeral after another since she had arrived, involving much toing and froing on coaches and trains, so she hadn't yet unpacked her usual wardrobe of pink and purple tops, and multi-coloured skirts. She wore dark clothes all the time, as though ready for the news of another death. In front of the mirror in the hall, before going out, over a loose black t-shirt and indigo jeans, she would put on a long black coat, buttoning it up, then fastening it with a leather belt against the cold. She was a black blur against the crisp white snow when she walked to the deserted bus stop, to wait for the bus.

Now, after yet another funeral, she felt quite empty, especially so near the presence of others' companionable excursions. People carrying bouquets and bottles, or marching off to war, with matching camouflaged kit. She had been there only a short time, too short to get to know anyone properly; not in England, where she had learnt apart from where sex was concerned, it takes years for people to say hello in the street, even if they live next door to each other for decades. And she knew England well, she had lived there almost all her life, and her life now went into a number of decades. She knew England and the English, or so she thought.

And although it wasn't that she had never been invited into other people's homes in that city – she had – but it was always around sex in the English way, drinking and eye contact, then going back to someone's place, albeit briefly. Another bottle and two glasses, talking as music plays, then going to bed, and leaving later – not sleeping – the curtailed promise and ending of romantic interludes. Never anything further, not even something like the beginning of a friendship, when she might walk along the street with a bottle and flowers in her arms, and wear another colour than black.

But then came an email: was she free for supper in a few weeks' time? She was, and she agreed. But then the day of the supper came, and in the morning when she went out to buy wine and flowers, she picked up the Saturday newspaper and realised from the headlines that it was the Eurovision song contest that night.

And later, in the early evening, crossing the grey commercial part of the city on route to the dinner party, the bus passed the turning to the more quaint and enticing Paradise Street, the tiny gay oasis in a city of straight married couples hosting dinner parties. On the corner, outside the Castle pub with its rainbow flag, people were smoking or swigging from bottles in the cheerful over-the-top hilarity of early evening drinking. There was a poster for that night's Eurovision dance-along-with-the-contest party. It reminded her of the over-the-top parties of other years, at London's Retro Bar, in pubs in Soho or at friends', all wearing colourful kitsch outfits and buzzing with energetic party gaiety. Sitting at high bar stools with girlfriends, or friends, arms around each other's shoulders, drinking the light bubbles of sparkling white wine. Or in the heat of sweaty, loud and boisterous proximity to others, but how beautiful to be on the dance floor, among kissing couples, scene queens striking a pose. To be in the midst of a relaxed group of friends, dancing, singing along, laughing – to be together.

Peering out of the window at the poster, she wondered how late the party would go on until. Feeling the tug of the small Castle crowd's exuberance, she stood for a moment. Would she get out of the bus, join the party? Remembering too, what she felt like in the company of the work colleagues with whom she was invited to spend the evening. That strange way the man's eyes screwed up into tiny creases when he focused on her; the way that the woman paused before answering, and then always objected precisely to whatever she had said. The bus doors clicked shut, and they started to move off, then swerved around the corner. She sat down, stretching out to clutch the plastic-bagged bottle from rolling off the seat, and the flowers, already starting to wilt.

Glancing back outside, she recognised a figure, one of her students from the term before. A misfit and yet a sociable character, hand-in-hand with a guy who was evidently another companionable misfit with a mismatched baggy outfit and bursting rucksack. In their shared isolation, from the beautiful city and its groomed inhabitants, they were absorbed in each other's company. As lovers do, they had eyes only for each other; they could have been in Venice or Venezuela; love's companionship releases us from time and place. In contrast she felt solidly there in that city, trapped on a bus with a bottle of warm wine and a bunch of dying flowers and an address to a middle class dinner party, somewhere not far, but a million miles from the Eurovision party. She wondered whether the drag queen from Vienna would win; she hoped so. Anything that would unsettle what she missed of London in this city's strange two-by-two-ness, its human Noah's Ark of heterosexuality. Like the Boden ads in the Sunday papers: healthy-looking identikit white, clothed, bodies.

When she was a child, dolls had white bodies. She would undress her dolls to see whether they looked like her underneath their synthetic clothes. But dolls don't have orifices, and there was something odd about a body without its built-in absences. Dolls weren't humans, but even so. Their mouths were set half open, but with no actual opening; they couldn't speak unless you spoke for them. There were dolls that if you pressed their tummies they would cry, but their lips didn't move.

And now she thought about how a doll's legs could be moved up and down or apart, but that in between a doll's legs where they joined the torso, there was just a flat surface. There was nowhere from which substances or objects could pass out or in. The place of sensation wasn't just sealed up: it was non-existent.

She walked down the street. The houses all looked alike, one after the other the doors were closed, and in front of them were identikit gardens, with a few feet of stone-slabbed path, then waist-height gates, locking in the few metres of space, greying greenery in the dusk, and sets of matching recycling and rubbish bins lined up, their lids closed.

Later, she cannot remember ringing the doorbell, the door being opened, or even being welcomed in. But she remembers the dinner party had already started as she entered: from down the corridor there were the high pitched tones mingled with lower deeper voices of middle class well-fed accents, glasses chinked in the smell and heat of English cooking, of cheese and fatty pastry. She felt like she was late, although she knew she wasn't, as she turned the corner into a room of people standing, juggling glasses and appetizer plates, like a scene from a play set in the thirties, not the twenty-first century.

And later, most of all what she remembers is strangely that she cannot remember much of what anyone said. Not even the extraordinarily precise manoeuvring around the long dining table, of where everyone was to sit, directed by the hostess with long pauses, looking at the person, the table, then directing them each in turn to sit in a particular position – as though the dining room was a stage set and they were actors, not guests at a dinner party. She was placed, not by the gay couple – the only guests she'd not met before – where she hoped she would be, but instead between two people she had the least in common with, although she quickly discovered she wouldn't be able to hear them anyway. As she sat down her back a few centimetres from the fan-oven, she was smothered by the oven's heat and its whirring noise, and the unpleasant smell of oozing fat, still lingering on her clothes hours later, on the return bus journey back through the city.

Had the evening been that bad? Perhaps not, but isn't conversation the point of a dinner party, people opening and closing their mouths – not just eating, drinking, consuming, but talking, conversing, communicating? And during all those hours from her hot spot at the head of the table there was only one phrase that someone spoke that stuck in her mind – and it was after hearing it that she wanted to get away, get quickly through the inevitable polite goodbyes, the 'we must do this again', while silently promising herself absolutely never again.

And that one phrase she remembers is 'Nice children,' said with a lick of the lips by the woman with the fruity elocutioned tones, hiding a childhood of no doubt another, perhaps lower classed, accent. And the phrase, now she remembers, was in the midst of the people around her talking of schools, a topic that seemed to concern the straight couples that predominated the party. 'Nice children' indicated that there were children who aren't nice.

Although she was new to the area she got the sense that what was being talked about was not the 'nice', but the not 'nice' kids. She had a sneaking suspicion that what was meant was the kids she had seen after four o'clock on the buses, laughing and frolicking joyfully after being released from silent schoolrooms – and more specifically, the kids with darker skin tones, like her own when she had looked down at her fingers placing the coffee cup down on the table, whilst shaking her head to the offer of another coffee.

Posters advertising the many private schools were dotted around the city. Their poster-children were silent, blonde, blue-eyed creatures; still images of static ghostly children holding tennis racquets but not playing, or sat at pianos, their fingers producing silence. One poster she had seen had a neatly uniformed Chinese girl, goggled up in a science lab. Kids could wear the same school uniforms, but underneath, like dolls, these adults seemed to imply that they were different to their own kids: that some children were permanently not 'nice'. Just like there are species that aren't human but animal, creatures that may overpower humans, for those adults there were other humans that seemed dangerous for 'nice' humans to socialise with, in case perhaps there was some bodily substance eventually transmitted. For them it was better to imagine others as dolls that can never speak, pee or make love.

The bus passes the Castle, its doors open on to Paradise Street, revealing rhythmic movement beneath coloured disco lights, bouncing and strobing, echoing similar lights from another pub further down the street. She wonders who had won. She looks towards the exuberance of the gay bars on a Saturday night, she misses London like she misses a lover, but she's on the last bus, it's too late to get off and join the party.

At the bus stop, just past the pub, as the doors are closing she hears some girls run on quickly, just in time. Tipsy, they make their way upstairs then past her on the top deck, straps slipping past their shoulders. The not 'nice' girls grown up, after a drink and a bit of a dance, chat at the tops of their excited voices, singing the winning song won by a man with a beard, dressed as a woman.

The night opened up – like a body with a mouth that opens to speak, suck, and kiss; like arms and legs that open, revealing nipples, breasts and orifices: stages promising creative acts, love-making, ecstasy, birth. Orifices that mark our entwined unsealed selves, without which our species will starve, fade and eventually die out.

The Picnic

SADIA IQBAL

Mrs Hussain wrapped the roasted chicken and paratha in foil; she prepared her flask with tea and emptied out a jar of mango pickle into a tiffin box. Her gold bangles jangled as she wiped down the counter and placed the foil packages into a wide bag. She draped her blue tasselled scarf around her head and pinned it in place.

The summer holidays were always difficult; the children grew bored in the house all day. Today, instead of waiting for their father to take them to the park, they had begged her to take them. She had given in because she wanted to make the most of the yellow days; there were so many grey days in this country.

Aysha, her twelve-year-old daughter watched her. 'Dad will want some of that chicken for his dinner.'

'We'll bring some back, if the boys don't eat it all', Mrs Hussain said.

'I reckon you will have to cook more,' Aysha said scrunching up her face at the mention of her greedy brothers.

They heard shouting coming from the front of the house. The boys often played there but the cramped space brought out their territorial side and they argued over every inch of space.

'Your brothers are fighting with each other again.'

'I'll sort them out,' Aysha said, as she hurried out of the kitchen.

Mrs Hussain now enjoyed a moment of silence, as she stood alone in her kitchen. On the wall opposite, next to the cupboard, she noticed her photograph was crooked, the nail bent, almost falling out. All three sisters were standing outside their father's clay house in Pakistani Kashmir. They wore Eid clothes: metres of glittery orange material on their girlish bodies, bare feet on the dusty ground, shy smiles. Her sisters had married men from nearby villages and she might have done the same if her father hadn't met Mr Hussain. He could read and write and had welcomed the offer from the British of a job in Slough. Her father had been overjoyed with the 'prosperous match'.

Mrs Hussain gently touched her sisters' face, lingering on her own now unrecognisable appearance through the glass frame and whispered a prayer.

'Come on mum,' Aysha called from the front door.

Mrs Hussain stepped out into the front garden and locked the door; her two boys, Mohammed and Musa were already waiting at the end of the path. As soon as they saw her, they opened the gate and ran off, kicking a ball between them.

'Be careful of the road,' Mrs Hussain shouted ahead. The thought came to her: children can run, they are still light.

Mrs Ali, the next-door neighbour was in her front garden picking up rubbish.

'Are you going to the park?' she said, watching the boys running.

'Yes,' Mrs Hussain said. 'The children won't wait for their father.'

'This generation of children can't wait for anything.' Mrs Ali said as she dropped a fistful of crisp wrappers into a black sack.

Both women smiled in their complete belief that they fully embodied the virtue of patience.

Mrs Hussain carried the picnic bag and walked slowly with Aysha. The sunlight fell onto the road as they walked across. Mrs Hussain felt glad of it, certain she had Allah's blessing. At the end of the road, there was an alleyway, where the boys knew to wait for her. It led straight into the park. She had never liked the alleyway. It often smelled of urine and young people with wild hair would lean against the inside fence and smoke charas. It reminded her of the dark path from her father's house to the water well where men loitered, knowing the women would pass to collect their daily water for cooking, cleaning and washing. They made obscene comments as they passed their smoke back and forth. So Mrs Hussain and her sisters pulled their scarfs over their faces to avoid their red eyes and the sweet earthy odour.

She had passed her fear on to Aysha, but then she was already afraid of so much; the smallest fluttering insects and the playful taunts of the local children. Her father would need to find a strong husband for her to lean against.

At the end of the passage, they stepped into the cheerful light of the park. Aysha and the boys took their ball to the flat grassy area. Mrs Hussain walked up to the wide bank. She laid out the blanket, sat down and watched her children. Here in the open space they played well together. Aysha shouted at Mohammed to run faster and block the ball from going into the goal. Then Mohammed and Musa lay on the wooden floor of the roundabout. Aysha held onto one of the red handles and ran along the side, pushing with her arms and legs, her green and yellow stripy scarf dancing behind her.

Mrs Hussain set out the food: she placed the chicken, parathas and pickle in the middle and put the paper plates around the edge. She called out to them. Mohammed and Musa came immediately and she handed them each a chicken leg. Aysha went over to the swings. She pushed her legs out and reached high towards the sky.

Mrs Hussain was biting into her paratha stuffed with pickles when she saw the two men come out of the alleyway. One of the men was tall, his tight trousers clung to his scrawny body and his head was shaved. The second man had a round belly like Mr Hussain and held a stocky black dog on a lead and smoked a cigarette. Both men were staring at Aysha; they exchanged a keen glance with one another. Mrs Hussain swallowed the mouthful of food.

The men walked to the swings. The skinny man sat on the empty seat next to Aysha. He lit a cigarette and glared at her. Aysha scraped her feet onto the ground to slow down the swing and looked over at the bank. Mrs Hussain couldn't quite tell but it looked like the skinny man said something. He then blew smoke in the direction of her daughter. The bellied man leaned against the metal frame and held the lead of his dog.

Mrs Hussain got up and launched her body forward, the momentum carrying her down the bank.

Aysha slipped off the swing and slowly backed away towards the roundabout. Mrs Hussain saw the familiar expression of fear on her daughter's face.

Aysha started to run.

'Dirty Paki bitch!'

The other man unhooked the dog's leash.

'Go on Rambo, get her,'

Mrs Hussain shouted, 'Aysha!' She turned back to her boys and said, 'Wait for me by the alley.'

Her daughter's green cotton salwar and kameez flapped around her small frame. Flap quicker, flap faster, flap, flap, flap.

The bellied man yelled, 'Go on!'

The dog leapt up and tore into her salwar. Aysha screamed as if she was being born.

'Bag-gy trou-sers, bag-gy trou-sers,' the men chanted triumphantly and made their way to the bank.

Mrs Hussain had barely walked anywhere, she now sweated with effort as she landed her body and pushed Aysha to the side.

The dog stared at the blue tassels swinging from side to side at Mrs Hussain's hips. Then Mrs Hussain grabbed the dog's thick neck; she tasted the dry heat of the Kashmir Mountain's and saw the shape of her mother's hands when she disciplined the guard dogs outside her father's house. In a quick action, she placed one hand on the bottom jaw, the other on top and opened it as wide as she could. Rambo's saliva spilled onto her fingers and down to her wrists and she smelled his metallic breath. She stared into his red brown eyes and heard her husband's words 'you stupid village woman, you know how to handle animals but not humans.' She shook the dog's square head from side to side and felt the pressure of his long teeth push into the palms of her hands. After a few seconds Rambo groaned, his jaw went slack and he turned around and ran towards the men. From the corner of her eye, Mrs Hussain could see the men were standing by her picnic. She wiped her hands on her scarf, then took Aysha's scarf and wrapped it around her small waist to cover the shameful hole across her thigh. Aysha began to cry quietly; she fiddled with the scarf to check it was still in place.

They both walked to the top of the alleyway and met the boys. Musa sobbed, 'mum, my ball, it's on the blanket.' He threw his little arms in the air and wailed.

'I will get it, wait here,' Mrs Hussain said. She could not bear for her little Raja to be upset.

Mrs Hussain saw both men were standing on the blanket, they had kicked the flask over and stomped on the parathas with their big boots. The dog was drooling over the chicken pieces, licking each one before settling on a leg.

'Leave,' the bellied man commanded as he watched the dog rip off a chunk of flesh.

'It's dirty.'

'Come,' he said waving the collar in the air. When the dog got close he pulled out the chicken leg.

'Good boy,' and put the collar back on Rambo. A few seconds later the dog picked up the chicken leg again, the man shrugged his shoulders.

'Paki bitch don't ever touch my dog again,' the skinny man said to Mrs Hussain as he put out a cigarette with his boot. She kept her eyes on the ground and surveyed the mess left on the blanket.

The men walked back down to the empty swings, the dog's tail curled at it's back.

Mrs Hussain quickly packed up, she wrapped the leftover chicken and placed it in her bag. She picked up the ball and hurried to meet her children at the alleyway.

The family walked through the alley in silence. Mohammed walked with one arm around Musa while Musa clutched his ball to his chest. Mrs Hussain stopped briefly to wipe their noses with her scarf, the tassels now stiff and sticky. She kissed the top of their heads and rubbed their small backs with her large hand, a touch of love to dull the prickly hate.

'Don't tell,' Mrs Hussain said. 'Or your father won't let me take you to the park again.'

Aysha who had been walking ahead, slowed down and walked next to Mrs Hussain. She linked arms and Mrs Hussain surprised at her daughters affection welcomed the action and took her daughters hand.

As they neared their house, she saw Mrs Ali was still tidying her front garden. It soothed her to see she was pulling up weeds that were choking the roses.

'How was the park?'

'The children ran a lot, they will sleep well.' Mrs Hussain said.

'Inshallah,' Mrs Ali said and returned to her weeding.

'Inshallah,' Mrs Hussain replied and walked into her house.

At the sink Mrs Hussain washed her hands and wrists as though she was preparing to read prayers. As she changed her scarf, she had a thought. She was confident it was a direct message from Allah. He told Mrs Hussain her light carefree days were in the past. She knew this truth; everything was heavy now including her. She had suffered when the cold claimed a part of her heart and made her body numb. It was her life in this country, a test and there would be rewards. She reached out to her photo and slipped it into the back of the cupboard where an unused sixteen-speed blender and toasted sandwich maker lived.

She returned to her sink and rinsed out the flask, she pulled the chicken out, the foil falling apart in her hands. 'Alhamdulillah,' she said as she quickly rinsed the chicken breast and leg, they were Mr Hussain's favourites. She would serve them to him for his dinner tonight.

The Boatboy
MONA DASH

Dhenkanal, Odisha, India, 1938

The river grew wide at this time of the year, increasing in girth every passing day. Baji liked to sit on the banks and watch her swell.

'She is big, she won't grow anymore,' his mother would say.

'If she remains like this for a few more weeks, the paddy fields will be full,' his father would hope. Together they would dream, a bountiful crop, food the year round; but that was when his father was still alive.

When Baji was only six years old, his father was claimed by a fever for days, then weeks. The kabiraja concocted a bitter paste to drink with water every night, the village priest visited to drive away the evil spirits. They assured he would be well soon. Instead, his father returned one evening from ferrying the boat, and collapsed. Baji reached out to touch him. His fingers recoiled, his father was stiff. He hadn't understood. His mother had started wailing, banging her head on the door of their hut. Within minutes, the villagers arrived. They had to take the body, they said. Someone carried Baji on his shoulders to the masani, the graveyard on the outskirts of the village. It was the duty of the son, however young, to light the pyre. The body laid on wood, some marigold flowers thrown on the coarse sheets, nothing elaborate – 'for we are not like the wealthy Raja or his Zamindars,'– his mother said.

It was seven years ago, yet he couldn't forget the heavy stick he'd been handed and advised to bring down hard on his father's head. 'It breaks the skull and lets the insides burn,' they'd explained. They wiped his tears, they gave him a banana to eat. For years he would remember how his father's hand had suddenly jerked up – they said it happened when the logs of wood burned and dislodged the body – burnt black, as if to say Bye-bye, ta-ta the way he did when he left for work in the morning. Ta-ta, and Baji would wave back until the boat grew smaller and the water still once more. Ta-ta.

#

The villagers worshipped Brahmani; calming her anger when she threatened to flood, praying for her waters to fill when there was a drought. The fields spanned their village Bhuban, then all the way upto the village of Ranpur.

Like the other boatmen, Baji's family lived on the banks of the Brahmani. His mother worked in the farmers' houses, grinding the paddy to husk. Baji went to school in the day, and in the afternoons, ferried the boat. The boatboy they called him. The villagers paid his mother with rice and grains. Sometimes he would catch fish; the silvery kokila flashing in the shallow waters, which his mother fried with salt, but only for him. 'Never, Baji, never!!' she shouted when he placed one small fish in the mound of rice she was eating. As a widow, she could only eat vegetarian food, cooked with no ginger, garlic or onion; it was as much a sin to offer non-vegetarian food to a widow, as it was for her to eat it, she explained. It seemed the whole world conspired to add to his mother's sorrows, Baji thought.

#

Once a month, the villagers were called upon to do bethi, work for the king, but with no wages. The palace on the hill, Yatna Mahal had been built through bethi. It had taken ten men five days to hang on the ceiling a decoration of lights and glass. It had come all the way from London, chand-elier they called it.

'But why should we work without wages?' When Baji asked his mother, she would panic, cover his mouth with her small hands, silencing him, 'He's the king, the Raja. We have to serve him.'

Once, the villagers were instructed to cook kheer for the king's palace. Baji and his friend Fagoo watched, eyes popping, – the milk from twenty cows, thickened, the rice soft – just once to slurp that milky, sweet thickness. They were not allowed a single spoonful.

'But why must we cook for them and part with our food?' he asked.

'So much trouble,' his mother whispered, 'you will get into so much trouble.' She sat him down and explained the laws of the land. Bethi was only of them. There was begari, when they had to carry the luggage of the British officials and Indian kings, free of charge. There was rasad, when they had to deliver goods, free of charge. They could do nothing to change these rules.

His mother wore a widow's white, the aanchal covering her head. Her large eyes shone, tears in them, as always.

'Why are you crying again, Bou?' he asked, at which she sobbed louder.

#

Baji looked at his reflection in the water, his bare body, the half dhoti, yellowish white, a bit tattered, tied firmly so that it didn't slip off. One day, he would leave Bhubhan, leave Dhenkanal district itself, and work in Cuttack. One day, he would wear a hat and coat, and speak in English. He would be a sahib, just like the Englishman, the Political officer of Orissa, who had come to their school last week.

They had prepared for the visit for months. On the day, the school was swept. The children came in clean clothes, faces scrubbed, hair brushed. They gathered for the assembly. Every child received a laddoo; Baji held the sweet, orange ball in his hand, wanting to save half of it for his mother. His bites were too big perhaps, for very soon nothing was left, except for the taste of sugar and ghee on his tongue.

The *sahib* was tall, his hair shone. He wore dark glasses, so that the sun didn't burn his eyes. In bilat, England, there was no sun; the moon lived in the sky permanently. In bilat there were no huts, everyone lived in houses, for there were no poor people. It was hard for the sahibs to come and live here, but they did. They were not used to the heat, the dirt roads. 'We have to look after them,' their teacher explained. So the boys did. They fanned the sahib, standing in a circle around the tall wooden chair he sat on. Major Bazelgette, they tried to say his name, the syllables falling of their tongues. 'Majjor Bajjelgette', 'a softer zzz,' the teacher instructed, but try as he might, Baji could only say, 'Bajjelgette.'

#

Nayantara, one of the village widows, lived with her parents, in the last hut, right where the bank sloped and the mud was even softer. Sometimes Baji saw her, sitting outside, in her white saree, feet draped in the water. Her husband had died a year ago and she had been sent back by her in-laws. Everyone had gathered, Baji among them, to watch her walk back into her parents' house, face lowered; her parents not happy with the returned guest. A daughter's place was with her husband and in-laws, after all. Everyone was commiserating with the parents, but no one seemed to notice that Nayantara's eyes were red, mouth misshapen, the way it was when you cried for hours. When he mentioned this to his mother, she nodded and said things would have been worse had Sati still been prevalent.

When Baji thought of Nayantara in flames, the fire burning her body just like it had burnt his father's, he could feel the fire in his nostrils.

Sometimes Fagoo came in the morning, when the sun was still feeble in the sky, and waited with him by the boat. One such day as they dug pebbles in the mud and flung them into the water, he nudged Baji. A slim body in the water, white saree sticking to her legs, Nayantara was swimming fast, furiously. Baji looked away, but Fagoo stood still and stared.

'Is she alright?' Baji worried. Was she trying to cross the river? Did she need the ferry?

'Sssh, of course she is fine. She is having her bath. I want to watch her.'

'You shouldn't.'

'Why not? Married at fourteen, widowed at sixteen, barren after two years, isn't that what they say about her?'

He wanted to do something which would silence Fagoo, make him look away from Nayantara's lithe form.

But just then, someone called out, 'Boatman! Hey, boy!'

At the sound of the voice renting the still air, Nayantara disappeared, a flash of white, a flash of brown and gone. She must have swum underwater, but Baji didn't see her resurface, and the three young men, were right there, ready to step into his little boat, talking animatedly all the time.

'You are the boatman, not him? Can you row us all across?' one of them asked, looking disbelievingly at Baji.

Fagoo was so much bigger than him, but he was fifteen, a year or more older than Baji.

'I can. I do this everyday,' he said.

Out of all the people he had ferried, there was something different about these men. Almost as if they stood straighter, their voices louder, none of the whispers he heard from the other villagers. Baji heard the word bethi a few times. He strained to hear better.

They came back the next day. One of them even smiled at Baji as he got off the boat.

Back and forth the river, a few times in the month. Who were they? Where did they go?

'Mohanty will join us, only a matter of time,' one of them said.

'Yes. We need more people like him. He refused to do bethi this month. They did a lathi charge, but he resisted. '

Baji, mustering courage interrupted, 'Can we resist? Can we refuse to do bethi?'

'Boy, what is your name?' the one with the moustache asked. His face was serious.

'Baji Rout.'

'And your father's?'

'He died some years ago.'

'By the king's orders, no doubt!' one of them laughed.

'We are – Baishnav, Raghu, Gobinda,' the other said pointing to himself and then the other two. 'We are sorry about you father. But that is what they do. They make us slave, we die, and they eat... and eat.'

Baji remembered his father, his thin frame standing firm on the boat as he rowed. The vest he wore with three holes, one much larger than the others.

'One day, Baji, it will all change. We will make it change!' Baishnav's eyes looked ahead, farther than where the river lapped on the other bank.

'Do you go to school?'

Baji nodded.

'Can you run an errand for us?' Rabi asked.

'One of our friends will come to the river bank tomorrow in the evening. Can you pass this note to him? He will come up to you and say 'hukum.' That's the cue.'

They gave him a whole anna and waved at him when they got off. Baji waved, Ta-ta, the coin tight in his fist. Hukum, order. Hukum, hukum he practised all the way home.

The next evening, a young man, wearing a khadi dhoti stood at the riverside. Baji knew it had to be one of them even before he said the word. He knew from the gait, from the look. They exchanged smiles.

#

'We will overthrow the Raja. The British are helping him and encouraging his practices. They will have to leave our country! We will be free.' Baishnav declared.

'But Bajelgette is so good, so kind. He talked to all of us,' Baji said.

The men laughed. 'Good?!!!They rule us, they are not of us. They need to go. The king needs to go. We, the people need to rule.'

'You will be king?' Baji asked.

'No, not I, Baji! We will rule, you, I, this will be our country!'

'But how?' Baji asked.

'We have to act together. In this struggle, everyone has a role. Even you, Baji, can help.'

Fire in their eyes, fury in their voices, bodies taut and straight, the wind streaming through their locks.

He told his mother about them, the brave founders of the people's movement, the 'Prajamandal.' The voice of the people against injustice, against the authority of the king.

'The Raja will become a common man and the British will finally leave! We will be free!'

'Ssshh, Baji,' his mother said.

'Hukum, Hukum,' he laughed.

#

Baji waited. The messages now arrived in the stillness of the night. The soft, barely there footfalls, the young man who held his hand out and passed a note, greenish paper folded tightly, then disappeared as quickly as he had arrived, from somewhere between the huts and trees. The next day, Baji would hand the note to a teacher in the school, no words spoken, taking care not to be seen, telling no one else.

The men praised him, patted him on the back. Sometimes they gave him two annas even. You are one of us, they smiled as the boat bobbed gently on the river. Someday it will all change, the promise was strong. India will belong to us, the people. The fire of freedom.

He felt like anything was possible. He felt like the time he had swum the river's breadth, cutting across the water faster than anyone else, then looking up, had seen Nayantara watching him. Surely her eyes were on him, surely she had smiled at him.

The next time his mother cooked fish, he counted four of the kokila, and clutching them in his closed fist, ran to the last hut. She was sitting outside the doorway, face blank, looking out towards the river. He held out in his hand, streaked turmeric, the crispy fried fish. She stared without a word, then looked back inside the hut hastily. For an instant he thought she would call out to someone, and they would come charging out. But in a quick motion, hardly touching his fingers, she grabbed them all and ran towards the riverbank. He followed, watching her hand move quickly to her mouth, her teeth chomping. She smiled at him, only at him.

He rushed back to his hut, heart pounding.

#

Baji stood on the banks, one night, the note in his hands, waiting. The river was swelling, the boat bobbed unsteadily. An unusually heavy rain for October. His mother would be so upset if she knew he was here standing in the dark, the moon hidden, drops dripping from his hair. But she slept deeply, the sleep of the tired.

Then he heard some footsteps, unmeasured, like some clumsy beast dashing through the forest.

Baji saw them, the police, their hats, their guns. Their brown uniforms, brown faces. Two hundred and twenty, the numbers would be written in history, rightly or wrongly, for posterity. He stood stolidly, feet wet, his heart knowing something would happen.

'Boy, take us across,' the first policeman said.

'We are looking for some men. We have burnt Ranpur down. Now it is the turn of Bhuban,' another shouted. There was a surge of laughter in the group.

Their rampaging was evident. Some looked dishevelled, blood spattered on their uniforms. They laughed and spoke in the language of the big city of Calcutta, Bengali. Baji had heard it once in school. It was said the sahibs had recreated London in Calcutta. Raja Singhdeo had been to Calcutta, even to London. The palace had photographs of the Raja in a carriage in London.

One day it would all change. One day. Even he, Baji could help.

'The Brahmani is full today. She doesn't want anyone to cross her,' he said, forcing his voice as loud as he could.

'Don't give us advice. Ferry us now. We have to go to the other side.'

'I will not.'

There was laughter. 'Do you know how to ferry a boat?'

'I do, but the boat is not for you.'

'The policemen shouted again, 'Get the boat out for us.'

Baji refused. One of the policemen came closer and shoved the bayonet against him. It struck hard on his shoulder. Another hit Baji's knee. He buckled, falling into the soft river mud, letting the note sink so it could never be found. Then, quickly scrambling up said, 'You can cross the river, only over my dead body.'

He had to stop them.

'Cross the river we will! Do you know Baishnav Patnaik and Raghunath Mohanty? Where are they?'

Baji knew Raghu bhai's blue kurta well, how he flicked his hair when he spoke. He knew how Baishnav bhai could swim across the river in ten minutes. He knew they had to live to lead them to the promised victory.

'No, I don't.'

The police looked at the rising waters. 'If they have jumped in, they will have died by now.'

Then again, 'Ferry us or tell us where they are!'

When he refused again, another policeman hit him. Right on the head, he felt the pain enter and descend into his body, weakening it. He fell, but this time the police restrained him, their feet on his chest, not letting him rise.

'Run, run, flee. They are here, looking for you! ' he shouted. A high, young boy voice over the rivers, a warning to whoever understood, whoever could hear.

'Prajamandala ra hukum nahin. I have no orders from the Prajamandal to ferry you. I only obey them.'

The police laughed louder. Baji felt them look at him, how many feet, how many guns over him? He would never know. The shots rang out, again and again.

#

With all the commotion, the villagers would gather and watch some of the policemen row themselves away in the boat, firing randomly as they went, killing three more men. The rest would storm through the village. Baji's mother would cry all night, her son's head in her lap. Baishnav, would arrive, anger storming his eyes and cradle Baji's thin, still body. Gobinda, Raghunath, Ananta and many others would summon the villages and together they would take Baji's and the other dead to Cuttack. People would leave their homes and join the procession, the masses swelling in broad daylight. A hero's farewell. They would sing when his pyre was lit, when the fire rose high in the skies – 'Nuhen bandhu, nuhen, eha chita, e desha timira tale e alibha mukati salita – Friends, this is not a pyre. This is the fire of freedom.'

Nayantara would sit alone on the bank for nights.

#

Some months later, Major Bazelgette would be killed by an angry group of protesting villagers. Nine years later, the villagers would be free, both from the King and the British.

India would achieve independence in 1947, but split into two, a scar remembered forever.

As for the boatboy, like so many others, he would barely be remembered, written about rarely, the youngest martyr of India.

The Boatboy is fictionalised but based on the life of Baji Rout, who died protecting his village. Baji lived in Dhenkanal, which was a part of the 'Garjat' area, the princely states of Orissa. Ruled by the kings, who were on the side of the British, the people of the princely states suffered under draconian rules and eventually rose in revolt. The police were on the side of the rulers, the king and the British. The people's movement, the Prajamandal was aided by the Congress. Baji died at fourteen, possibly the youngest martyr of the country but very little is found about him outside his home state of Odisha, India.

The words 'Nuhen bandhu, nuhen, eha chita, e desha timira tale e alibha mukati salita' are from the poem, 'Baji Rout,' by Sachi RautRay, an award winning poet from Odisha.

Mind the Gap
FARRAH YUSUF

Mother's anger entered a room before she did. Prowling around with such stealth it was almost invisible to all but me. As Mother herself entered, it beckoned her over and whispered in her ear. A deal was done and more often than not a victim had been sought. When I was eight, I decided to name it Henry. So tightly was Mother cloaked in Henry's spell that everything she saw was filtered through his lens.

Henry was born on Tuesday 19 July 1994 at 6:13 pm – exactly the same time as my Minnie Mouse digital watch froze. Along with my homework on the Tudors, my watch hit the wall the moment Henry came forth. Pages sprayed and screen cracked they both lay on the floor while Henry dared me to collect them. From then on, Henry was the closest I ever came to having a sibling.

Much like his kingly namesake, you didn't argue with Henry. I tiptoed around the house trying to avoid him but our paths couldn't help but cross. Had he been a colour he would have been red, like the ruby in the wedding ring Mother never took off, but he had no fixed colour or form. Henry grew at a much faster rate than I did. By the time I was in my early teens he had the strength of a man and he overshadowed the Mummy I had once known.

Mother fed Henry on the silence Father left. Missing was the word everyone used. Initially, the police whispered it when they saw I was around. Before long however it became part of his name – Mr James Vincent Sawyer. Missing. Closely followed by, Mr James Vincent Sawyer – Missing – age 29, last seen at approximately 7.15 am on Thursday 14 July 1994 leaving his home in Walthamstow, North London.

Nooni and I became as inseparable as Henry and Mother. Nooni arrived three weeks after Henry's birth and a month after my ninth birthday. Her caravan lurched into our driveway before coming to a permanent halt. No sooner had she arrived Henry told her to leave. Try as he might she would not go back to her cottage in Kent, neither would she invite him into her new dome shaped home. Unlike Mother she refused to be his host. I should have called Nooni Nana but having mixed Noreen and Nana I made Nooni and it stuck. Henry was not scared nor was he fond of Nooni, which meant that she was all mine.

Father left while Mother was in the shower and I was meant to be in bed. He took the car but left his house keys on the stairs and his jacket on its usual peg. No note, no goodbye, no nothing. He just woke up that day, put on his clothes and left.

They had been together since they were sixteen. They'd met while working in a café called Borders because half of it was in Islington and the other in Hackney. I'd come along when they were barely twenty. He'd given up playing with his folk band and got a job in a factory because a baby and rent was more expensive than they had thought. He sold all his guitars because he didn't like to see them lying around and took up gardening instead. Sometimes he said he missed his band and sometimes he said he was glad because he loved me more than music. He told me every night I was the best thing in his world.

I watched him go. Leaving me behind. He lied or he'd have taken me with him. Later Mother asked me about it again and again. I told her the little I saw. I woke up early as I needed to pee but with Mother in the bathroom, I waited in bed. I opened my curtains just as he was slipping into his car. I tapped on the window and waved but he didn't even look up at me. He just started the engine and turned left. Every time Mother made me repeat it I wondered what I could have done or if I remembered it wrong. It was only when nosey old Mrs Lee, from four doors down, said she had seen him too that Mother stopped asking me. Maybe it was my fault. Maybe if it wasn't for me he wouldn't have gone. Maybe he missed his guitars more than he loved me.

Mother sent me to school with the neighbours while she began ringing Father's work, followed by all our family and friends and even his old bandmates. When Mother was late to collect me the teachers told me to wait by the staff room until she came. When she finally arrived, there was no sorry, no cuddle, no treats to eat. We walked home in silence as she fiddled with her ring and I thought I saw the ruby wink at me.

That weekend went by in a haze until the moment a policeman called to say they had found Father's car not far from he grew up on Ridley Road. A man had seen some teens break into it and steal the radio so he alerted the police. Father, however, was nowhere to be seen. Once the car was found a word that entered our lives and never left was CCTV. Mother and CCTV became unwilling best friends. Sometimes she would go alone to watch it. Sometimes Uncle Tony, Father's younger brother, went too. They would leave tense and come back in tears. They sat with Nooni and debated for hours where he could be. I sat silently on the stairs listening and wondering if he was playing at gigs or reading bedtime stories to another daughter he loved more than me or if he didn't like Mother's neon pink lipstick anymore. Uncle Tony and Father could not look less alike but they sounded like brothers and I wished he wouldn't speak. His voice annoyed me.

The initial flood of family, friends and visiting noisy neighbours, became a trickle before running dry as the months went by. For Mother all clocks stopped the day Father left as if for us time had been reset but for others it moved on and we were left on our own.

Until one day a local journalist knocked on our door with question after question about where Father was. Rather than roar, Henry went to sleep and one of his friends came instead. This time it was tears but sometimes it was sadness or despair. Eventually the journalist left and Nooni sent me to get every paper I could find from Mr Gupta's shop on the corner of our street. When I entered Mr Gupta stood behind his till sipping tea, in front of him was a stack of papers plastered with Father's face. He looked at me with such pity I wanted to scream. I wanted to say I don't care he isn't my Father anymore. Instead I paid quickly and left with as many papers as my rucksack and arms would hold.

The headlines claimed Father was wanted in regard to a robbery but the police never called. Two days later when the paper realised they had made a mistake they issued an apology. This time it wasn't a front page headline it was just a small box somewhere between the ads and obituaries. When I pointed it out, Henry was quiet and Nooni hugged Mother tightly for what seemed like hours on end.

After that, I decided I wouldn't speak about Father unless I was with Mother or inside our house no matter what anyone said or asked me. I'd stay quiet until they got bored. Mother on the other hand decided we had to do more to look for him because no one was taking us seriously.

Since Father left, weekends were no longer time for fun or trips to the park with friends. Come rain or shine, Saturdays were for gardening as that was Father's favourite pastime. No matter what Nooni said, Mother was adamant the garden had to be maintained for when he came home. There was one guarantee which I clung onto all week, Henry would be asleep while Mother weeded, mowed, and pruned until sunset. Saturday nights on the other hand Henry awoke ready for action as soon as an opportunity arose.

Saturdays nights were always the same. Preparation for Sunday - Poster Day. No more Sunday roasts with gravy and crispy potatoes without their skins, only tuna sandwiches, wrapped tight in cling film and a thermos of tea. As soon as Mother was done gardening she began to clean the car. The same car Father had deserted near Ridley Road. People must have passed him as he parked it and walked away but no one noticed or thought twice about who he was or where he was going. The police found no witnesses and the angle of the nearest CCTV camera was inches away from where the car had been. Mother insisted we kept the car as if it were a key to the life that could have been.

Our Saturday night ritual began with printing fresh posters of Father's face. Mother had bought a computer and printer especially. Once the posters were dry and had been placed in plastic sleeves, ready to go on poles and in shop windows, we loaded them in the car along with sticky tape and string. Henry watched my every move while Mother plotted the route for our latest trip to whenever any stranger had said Father may have been seen.

Sunday mornings too always began the same way, Henry and Nooni would scream at each other while I sat in Nooni's caravan. Nooni insisting I should stay home and Henry insisting I must go or else I might forget Father. They didn't realise that I tried every day to flush him from my thoughts. I couldn't risk feeling like I did the day he left. Mother made Nooni stay home for she would never let the house be empty in case he came back. Now I see, Nooni agreed for the same reason I went - to keep Henry from feeding further on Mother's soul. I learned early on to only wear trainers, never shoes, for we would walk for miles till

Mother felt that the day's work was done. If passers-by had stopped to look Henry would be good and if they hadn't Henry made it a long drive home. I kept my eye on the ruby all day to see how Henry was doing so I knew how to act.

Weekdays rolled on, hopes rising and falling with any scrap of news. The landlord kept putting up the rent so Mother took on double shifts at the Post Office which meant for five days of the week it was just Nooni and me. Nooni tried to say Mother was doing it to help ends meet but I knew the truth - it was to avoid me. Mother slept in the evening when I was back from school so Nooni and I crept around until it was time for her night shift. Once she was gone we were free to use the toaster, turn on the TV and anything else that made a noise. I wasn't sure if I missed Father but I knew I missed Mother more. Nooni and Mother had similar hands and if I squinted I could pretend it was Mother tucking me in.

Nearly a year after he left, we drove to Birmingham to visit a suburb where an unconfirmed sighting had been. As we passed through a high street, Mother stopped the car in the middle of the road and jumped out.

'James, Jaaaaaaaaaaaaaaaames!' she screamed.

I watched her run down the road as the traffic behind me began to beep and beep till I thought my head might explode. Unsure what to do I jumped out in pursuit. The second I had hesitated meant I was too late. She had been swallowed up in the sales chaos and was nowhere to be seen. I walked around and around until I noticed fingers and stares pointing towards a bench. There she sat shaking, her face in her hands, as I sat down beside her she looked up and said,

'I was so sure it was him.'

I looked at the ruby which had taken on a greyish tinge as if a light within it had dimmed. Mother and I got back to the car just as it was about to be towed. Henry was frozen and Mother was still so I was left to plead with the traffic warden but it was too late, a large fee had to be paid. After that, Mother began to drive slowly wherever we went. Staring at strangers hoping Father's face would emerge. Her illusions led to chases that ensured that ticket after ticket came through our front door. Mother placed them along with other unopened post on the left hand side of the sofa, where Father had always sat. Every few days Nooni would steam the latest ones open and start making calls and writing as many cheques as her pension allowed. Once finished she would gently place them back before her daughter came home.

Christmases, Birthdays, Anniversaries came and went without a word. Henry slept while Mother spent them staring out the window, watching, waiting, in hope. Nooni always took me to her caravan so we could be alone. She would draw down the blinds and we would listen to the radio and knit or sew. In winter she would make hot chocolate with marshmallows and in summer pink lemonade. By nightfall, Henry often stirred and began to bellow before getting tired and going back to sleep. Once

Nooni had checked all was clear I would tip toe up to my room and rock myself to sleep.

Some days Henry and Mother did not get along. They would fight and he would retreat. On those rare occasions there would be fish fingers, chips and if I was very lucky baked beans instead of peas. He never stayed away for long though and on his return, as if charged up from his rest, he and the ruby were at their brightest.

One day I caught Mother looking at her wedding photos. There was no Henry for once, I could see that in the dullness of the ruby. It was just Mother and me. Without looking up she said, 'Do you think he will come back? He belongs with us.'

How could I say, 'no Mother I don't' and 'he didn't think that or he wouldn't have left' so I just stayed silent and let her be.

'We're a family. He is meant to be here.'

I sometimes wondered why she'd never tried meeting anyone else. Nooni said it was because she thought they were meant to be, that they were soulmates or something like that.

She kept looking at the photos as if they would make him come back.

'He wouldn't just leave us like that. Without a reason or a note. He just wouldn't. Something must have happened. He wouldn't do that.'

She paused before continuing, 'Where can he have gone? He's alive. I know. I would feel it if he wasn't.'

She began to pass me photos taken at my birth.

She whispered, 'You see he was so happy. There was no sign. No hint he might go.'

I piled them up without looking, for I had seen them before.

'I thought we were happy. I thought we had a life. I thought I was a good wife. I don't understand. They say he may have been having an affair or have another family. A double life. They say he may have been depressed. Or he may have killed himself or lost his memory. I don't buy it. I don't. I don't.'

I sat silent for a moment knowing Henry was about to appear for the ruby turned from rosy to a deep red, as if it were ready to bleed, and Mother jumped up from her seat.

Henry began to rip up the photos and scatter them in the air before furiously collecting them only to do it again and again. Nooni stood in the hallway crying as Henry began ripping at Mother's clothes.

The next day, I tried to kill Henry but I killed Mother instead. I didn't need a knife or a gun I just showed her a letter that had come in the post. It said that Father could now officially be presumed dead.

Cows and Lambs
LYNNE E. BLACKWOOD

Broken planks and withies lay scattered over the trampled grass. Nandi rubbed his eyes in disbelief then stared in dismay at the empty corral. Where had they gone?

Cows weren't in the habit of breaking out like that unless…a tiger? Had they been so terrified as to smash his handiwork to smithereens and run off in panic? Nandi swung his head around in all directions but couldn't see signs of the animals. Not one tip of a long horn peeked from forest vegetation or tea plantations; not a swish of a tail nor a distant moo were to be heard nor the sound of hooves shifting in undergrowth. His worried eyes scanned the grass around the empty corral and towards the forest entrance were a tiger would drag their prey. No blood, no browning of grass scraped from the roots by the weight of a dead carcass, or, Shiva forbid, the gory traces of a terrified animal struggling in the feline's enormous paws.

Nandi passed his forearm over his sweating brow and smelled the lingering scent of his wife's patchouli oil. The baby. He'd forgotten about the morning milk. She would need it when dawn broke and his five cows were nowhere to be seen. He had to find them but where had they gone? Perhaps it had been an elephant that had trampled the enclosure? There was a rogue bull in the area but Nandi doubted it would come this high up the exposed slopes striped with rows of tea-bushes. Or maybe a bull *gaur* excited by Nandi's domestic cows had raged out of the forest, nostrils flaring? That would have spooked the cows and those wide, powerful shoulders and horns were capable of destroying his enclosure in no time at all.

He moved swiftly to where the gate should have been, now lying in splinters and inspected the grass closely around the smashed corral. Yes, the trail appeared to lead down the slopes past the tea plantations and into the valley towards the town. He followed the crushed vegetation for a few yards and discovered the fresh, tell-tale cow-pat, still steaming faintly - but also a smaller turd nearby. Wild dogs, those crazy feral animals the English had brought, lost and left to form roaming packs that threatened even a man if he found himself in their way. A pack must have come out of the forest. He felt so angry and as he craned his neck to see down the slopes and over the thickets of rhododendrons, suddenly felt fear. His stomach twisted as he gazed down into the deep valley.

The English. If his cows trespassed into their valley and the cleared swathes of land they used to assemble for fox-hunting, his precious animals would be killed or confiscated and his livelihood would disappear forever. Nandi froze and swallowed the saliva rushing to his mouth as he noticed several dark dots on the common and made out the silent arrival of a carriage and some horsemen, all tiny specks in the distance but clear enough to boost his adrenaline and make Nandi run at full speed back to their hut. He grabbed his herder's stave and halted in front of the flimsy wooden door, opening it very gently, pulling it up slightly on the leather hinges to prevent it scraping the beaten earth, all the while gulping down heavy breaths that heaved from his lungs.

His wife sprawled sound asleep on their pallet, her plump arms enclosing the baby. Nandi noticed the sheen of sweat on her brown skin. The sun wasn't completely up but heat was setting in for the day. The smell of yesterday evening's bamboo shoot curry still lingered, mixing with sweet patchouli. His home and family needed the cows.

Nandi tiptoed over to the other pallet and sharply prodded his son with the stave.

'Gujja, Gujja,' he hissed in a stifled whisper through betel-red teeth. 'Get up boy.'

His son sat upright, rubbed his fists hard into the sockets and stared at his father with eyes still bleary from sleep.

'*Appa*, father?' he questioned. 'Why so early?'

'Get up silently and come with me now.' Nandi bent and roughly grabbed Gujja's upper arm to pull him off the pallet.

'Why? Where are we going?' the child mumbled.

'Don't ask, just come with me.'

Gujja rose unsteadily on his feet, stretched his arms and let out a noisy yawn.

'No noise! Don't wake your mother or your sister and *not* the baby.' Nandi hissed as he frantically pulled the child, stumbling, out of the hut and slowly replaced the latch on the door behind him.

Gujja blinked several times against the morning light, then protested as sleep finally left his brain. 'Where are we going, *appa*?'

'Look hard. What do you see?' and Nandi spread his arms wide towards the broken enclosure.

'The cows aren't there anymore?' Gujja ventured.

'Cows have fled down into the valley and we must bring them back before the English begin their hunt. What can you see down there, eh? Tell me now?'

Gujja stood on tiptoes and tipped his body to peer through a break in the rhododendron thicket. 'They come to hunt? This early, *appa*?'

'Of course, now take your stave and come with me quickly.' Nandi began to trot in the direction of the tea plantation and down the steep slope towards the thickets and lush vegetation.

'But *appa*,' Gujja cried out after his father, 'I'm in my *dhoti*, I need my robe and must go wash my mouth out.'

Nandi stopped in his tacks and turned back to Gujja. 'Am I in my robes? Do you see me taking my time to wash my mouth out, to pray to Shiva? The cows, Gujja, the cows, we need to find them before they get slaughtered or even stolen. The English have already stolen our land. The cows are all we have left. Come now and fast or I'll be by your side in an instant and beat you with my stave.'

Gujja tightened his loin-cloth and ran, tripping and stumbling until he reached his father. Gujja looked down. '*appa*, I don't have my sandals to run all the way down there.'

'Run with me now and forget about your sandals. You're not going to that Missionary school, boy. You're a Badaga son helping his father and family. Bare feet will do. It will harden you.'

Gujja stared, rooted to the spot as his father set out at a fast trot. He looked again at his bare feet and then, ran again, as fast as he could, this time to follow Nandi.

Nandi was forging ahead and running alongside the tea bush rows, down the cleared land and towards the rhododendron thickets. Gujja's spindly legs raced after his father down the steep slopes the best he could but the child began panting as he lost his breath. Gujja halted and clutching at one side of his ribcage, bent over to catch his breath before calling out to Nandi.

'*appa!*'

Nandi halted in his tracks. 'What now?'

'I have stitch.'

Nandi looked back up the hillside at his son and shook his head.

'What 'stitch'?'

'Pain in side of chest when I can't breathe. It is English word, *appa.*'

A red flush crept under Nandi's tanned skin.

'English words now? Do you have a needle and thread in your skin? Has your mother sewn something into your body? 'Stitch'? Stupid. Come along quickly or I'll bring my stick to you. The cows, Gujja, the cows.' Nandi waited an instant as Gujja straightened and began to trot hesitantly towards him. 'Faster. The cows can't wait.' then sped down towards the path through the thickets.

Gujja concentrated on maintaining a regular speed to follow his father into the thickets but as Nandi disappeared into the tall shrubs, he was obliged to run faster, his bare feet now thudding uncomfortably on dried twigs, branches and vegetation that filled the narrow path. Leaves and branches thrashed his face as he plunged through the bushes; his arms were scratched and bleeding but Gujja ploughed on in his father's wake. The cows, the cows, he repeated to himself, hoping deep down that the animals would be found soon. The soles of his feet burned.

Gujja emerged from the thicket gasping for breath. His father waited several yards ahead, kneeling over and scrutinising a grass tuft.

'Come son. Tell me what you see here.'

Gujja set his legs into action but stubbed his toes on a pile of rocks in his haste and flew flat on his stomach into the long grass.

Nandi jerked his head at Gujja's cry and leapt to his feet. He ran to his son's side and knelt down. 'Gujja, my son, are you hurt?' The scent of crushed grass filled his nostrils as he gently turned Gujja over onto his back. Nandi saw the scratches on the bare body, the cuts on the soles of his feet and pulled his son to his chest.

'The cows, *appa,* the cows.'

Nandi sighed with relief at the dazed boy's mumblings and stroked back the dark hair from Gujja's clammy forehead. 'Come, son. I will carry you on my back a little way.' Nandi lifted the child onto his back and hooked his arms under the boy's knees. 'Hold tight onto my neck, now,' and continued his descent towards the valley and the growing number of specks that now dotted the green carpet below. The cows, the cows, he mumbled with anxiety.

They were now on the hillock looking over the last stretch to the valley and Nandi stopped.

'Get down now and tell me if you see anything.'

Gujja clambered off his father's back and lifted a hand to shield his eyes from the rising sun's glare.

Nandi didn't want to admit it, but he could see things far away more easily than nearby. His sight wasn't as good as it used to be and Gujja often served as his father's sight. Except when the boy was at that school. Not that he had any choice. The Governor had signed a compulsory education order and all the children, whether Toda, Badaga, Malayam or Hindu attended each morning to learn English, to read and write and arithmetic. Nandi couldn't see the point of it all. How were the parents supposed to tend to their fields and livestock if the children were absent? And what about usual chores such as fetching water or minding younger siblings?

'*appa,* I see the cows.'

'Where are they, Gujja?' Nandi raised invisible hands to Shiva in the sky and prayed the animals were in the last thicket and not the valley near the road.

'On the road, *appa.*'

Nandi groaned and shook his head. 'How many people are in the valley? Are there many more?'

'Oh yes, *appa.* The valley is full of people now. There are many carriages and sulkies and I can see dozens of people on horses. There are so many people, *appa.* What shall we do?'

Gujja lifted his face streaked with grime and sweat to his dumbstruck father. 'The cows, *appa,* the cows.'

'Yes, we must go and fetch them, son, before the English begin hunting. Come with me but stay close and don't talk out of turn, remember.'

As father and son descended the last stretch of rhododendron thicket, they both suddenly stopped to listen. From behind the hillock and further down the road in the direction of the barracks the sound of music drifted towards them with the breeze.

Nandi looked puzzled. 'What instruments make such a sound, son?'

Gujja's face lit up. 'An army band, *appa.* It is splendid and the uniforms all braided with gold and silver buttons. The school took us once and you should see those metal horns with pistons you press to make the sound. It's not a hunt!'

'And our cows are standing in the middle of the road, Gujja. Look!' Nandi pointed to where his animals waved long horns and swished tails in all serenity in the middle of the road lined with English.

'Come with me, *appa*. I have my stick and you have your stave. We can go quickly and try to move them off.' Gujja leapt down the embankment in a couple of bounds. 'Sorry, sorry, sorry,' he repeated in English as he wiggled a path through the crowds.

Nandi followed at a hesitant pace. He wasn't certain of the reaction so politely bowed his head and muttered excuses in Badaga, trying not to touch people. Most pulled away in disgust and surprise at his audacity but Nandi repeated in his head – 'The cows, the cows, my family needs my cows.'

Gujja was already whacking rumps when Nandi finally put his feet on the road. They began herding the obstinate animals towards a clear space near the verge when the music suddenly broke the air.

From around the bend rode a dozen soldiers in bright uniforms, followed by the musicians. Behind them, as far as the eye could see, were lines and lines of marching soldiers, Indians from every corner of the land, all in khaki uniforms, the only distinguishing feature being the headgear. Some with turbans, some Sikhs, some with Gurkha hats, others with British Army caps.

Nandi froze as hooves clattered to a standstill, less than a couple of yards from him, his son and his precious cows.

'What do we have here,' a brightly uniformed officer bellowed from atop his horse. 'Out of our way, you savages.'

The officer pulled his gun from the holster and aimed towards the animals.

'Sir, sorry sir,' Gujja said, head bowed, his whole body shaking.

Nandi stood, stave raised, unable to move, as he heard his son dare speak up. No good will come of this, he thought.

'I am very sorry, Sir. A tiger frightened our cows but we can move them quickly if you allow,' Gujja continued in English.

The officer's hand was pushed to one side by another as he urged his horse forward.

'Put that away, Lieutenant. No need for that here.'

Gujja felt the horse's hot breath snorted from the nostrils towering above him but stood his ground. The thought of saving the cows overrode the fear he felt.

'So, little man. You speak English very well.'

'Yes, Sir, I go to school every morning and learn.'

Gujja heard the creak of well-oiled leather as the officer inclined lower over the saddle.

'Well done, boy. We need young ones like you to join the army. Some education can take you far, you know.'

Gujja dared raised his head. 'I think I will when I am grown, Sir. But I want to be an officer like you and go fight for the King.'

The officers all guffawed in unison. Nandi blanched. He looked on at his son speaking English and felt a nudge of admiration for the boy. But what was he saying to make the

English laugh so loud? Nandi began to worry. Should he speak to Gujja? Or wait and see what would happen?

'And what's so funny?' the officer shouted above the laughs. 'The boy has ambition and we need Indians like him in our ranks.'

Instant silence fell at the reprimand. Horses champed, snorted and the shuffle of arms being adjusted and soldiers shifting in the ranks snaking back along the road to the barracks were the only sounds as Gujja waited. Nandi too – with bated breath.

'We are going to war, boy, and you are too young for now. The next time perhaps? This one will be over in no time.'

'Are you going to France,' Gujja enquired.

'Yes we are. How do you know that?'

'I read the India Times at the Missionary school, Sir and all about the war against the Kaiser.'

The officer stared intently at Gujja. 'You are certainly a bright boy. What do you know of the war over there?'

Gujja hesitated. It wasn't very good and he had already heard of villagers who had been killed. He knew the Indian units were always placed in the front lines. Should he be honest with this kind Englishman? He held his breath and felt his chest tighten.

'Many casualties, Sir.'

The officer sat straight in his saddle and frowned. Then he bent further down to Gujja and murmured so only they could hear.

'I was born in India, boy, and don't know anything about Europe. What I do know is I have orders to lead my men like lambs to the slaughter and it doesn't sit well with my conscience. Keep up with school and endeavour to become an officer. Our generals will need soldiers like you in future wars. What is your name?'

'Gujja, sir.'

'Well, Gujja, tell your father over there to take that terrified look off his face and say to him from me that I think he has a most courageous and intelligent son who he should be proud off. Now try and move your animals as quickly as possible. I must march my men to battle.'

Gujja gulped. 'Yes, Sir, I will Sir, and thank you.'

'Thank me for what, may I ask?'

'For the advice, Sir. I learn a lesson from you for when I will be an officer – never lead my men like lambs to the slaughter.'

The officer laughed, reined in his impatient horse and turned back to his men.

'*Appa,* we can move the cows but quickly,' Gujja shouted to Nandi and began tapping rumps to herd them towards the steep verge.

Once safely up onto the slope and the cows following the right direction towards home, Nandi stopped.

'You spoke a lot of English back there, son. What was so interesting for you to have a conversation with an Englishman?'

'He told me things, *appa.*'

Nandi stabbed his stave into the earth with impatience. 'What things?'

'You should be proud of me. He said the army needs officers like me and to carry on with school.'

'Hmmm,' Nandi grumbled, begrudgingly admitting that school could be a good thing after all. It had saved his cows. If Gujja hadn't spoken English and had a conversation with the officer, the outcome might have been different – disastrous, even.

'So you won't be a Badaga cow-herder like me, then?'

Gujja turned and looked his father up and down. '*appa*, I will always be Badaga and a cow-herder but I will be a good officer who won't lead his soldiers like lambs to the slaughter.'

Under the Same Sky
FARHANA KHALIQUE

I just wanted to see the stars.

One would do. It didn't even have to twinkle. It could be cold and chalky, like a full stop on a blackboard.

Not a distant bulb, or an airplane, or a bug. An actual star. Then I could stop shivering at my window and go back to bed. Even though I couldn't sleep and I'd be up again in a few hours.

Just one star. Burning away, light years from here, already dying, maybe already dead.

At least I'd know it was real.

#

I was looking at stars when we first met. It was twenty years ago, that day in Year Five, when you joined our primary school. Do you remember? We were having a science lesson one January morning, answering questions on The Human Body. As usual, I was doing my best to *keep-my-head-down*. But, as usual, I'd flick through the textbook to peep at the chapter on Space. There were pictures of different stars, including one of the Orion Nebula. I'd always look at that, such luminous pinks and blues, like strewn sherbet. It was the prettiest thing I'd ever seen, but kinda scary too.

That's when you joined us. *Ooh, New Girl,* we Chinese-whispered and craned our necks. You flushed, but stuck out your chin and stared back. You didn't have a school uniform yet, but you had perfect navy pleats, a crisp blue shirt and a cocoa-coloured face with large eyes and neat braids. Even your hair bobble was blue. Miss Cox chalked 'Sophie' on the board, then said you should sit next to... She looked around and Lula, the tallest, sat ramrod straight with a saccharine smile, but Miss' eyes settled on... 'Najma'.

Me? I froze and Lula slumped, the same expression on her face as she had once when I wouldn't let her copy my English work. *No, not me.* Lula was better, she was as loud as a siren and loved telling people what to do. Or Jimmy, whose red hair was as bright as his smile. Or Fairooz, who wore big round glasses and spoke so much that she never gave you a chance to be speechless. *Why me?* I was just the quiet Bangladeshi girl with the long plait and sensible shoes, who just wanted to *keep-her-head-down*, who knew nothing about the O.J. Simpson trial, who didn't care if Robbie might leave Take That, who wasn't watching Brookside, and who knew nothing about sitting next to a New Girl.

But you just shrugged off the stares and came and sat down. I pushed my textbook nearer to you; a tentative offering. You looked at the book, then at the numbers on the board, then raised your eyebrows. *Oh!* My turn to flush, *I was on the wrong chapter!* Then you smiled, pointed at the nebula and whispered, 'That's pretty!' then discreetly turned to the correct page. My eyes widened, then I beamed back.

#

To be honest, I was a New Girl once. It had only been two years earlier that Mum and my brother and I were parcelled off from Bangladesh to England. Dad had been beavering away in the curry houses here for the last few years so that he could establish himself and then bring us over. London was just as damp and grey and noisy as Sylhet had been lush and green and quiet. But I liked the flat above Dad's restaurant and I was relieved that I'd gone to an international school, which meant that my English wasn't bad. So, when I joined Lula and the others, I thought I might slip in without a ripple. Then I wrote a poem in simple, but perfect rhyming couplets and the teacher read it aloud and stuck it up on the wall. Lula, all smiles, grabbed my arm and wanted to know all about it at playtime. I smiled back, but her questions soon turned sour. She asked loudly, as the other kids gathered around, why I spoke with a fake American accent. Then, when she found out that I lived above a restaurant, her eyes gleamed.

'Oh! So your house stinks of curry.' A wave of titters hit me like a slap and Lula stepped closer. 'Actually, so do you.'

I froze and stared blindly, the other bodies one heaving mass of heat.

'Curry Girl!' Lula hissed. Then she turned and walked away.

The name stuck, and in the following days and beyond I buried the idea of making any friends here and told myself to just *keep-my-head-down*. Maybe one day it would work.

#

Then you came along and sat next to me. So, as your Buddy, I thought I'd at least show you around. I knew: which days school dinners were edible and which days to bring packed lunch; the safest place to cross the playground to avoid death by football; where to stand under the arches that covered the far side of the playground if you wanted to scoff sweets; which kids had spare stationery; and which kids to avoid lending anything. You: were all the way from Ghana, but spoke perfect, unaccented English; were a natural at Double Dutch; already knew the times-tables; and were the only one who didn't walk to school or get dropped off by a parent.

'You get a bus to school? *By yourself?*' Lula loomed over us one playtime, but all the kids in our class were open-mouthed.

'It's just one bus.' You shrugged. Lula looked like she wanted more, but someone mentioned Brookside and Trevor Jordache and the patio again, and everyone dispersed.

You added later, under the arches, 'Well, it's not like I have any choice.' That's when you told me about the council placing you and your mum in Mitcham, but East Hill being the nearest school with a space. And about your parents' separation. And about your mum being a shift worker at the hotel. In contrast, I said my parents were firmly married, but Mum had once thrown a plate of rice and curry at Dad. There was still a smudge on the wall where she'd missed.

Impressed, you'd asked me if there'd been Another Woman too, but I said, 'Nah. She wasn't feeling well and he'd tried to cook instead.'

#

Winter melted into spring. The boys played Eric Cantonas karate-kicking Crystal Palace fans, the girls crooned along to Take That's Back for Good, and you and I settled into an orbit. School was a steady stream of projects and playtime, with the occasional trip to the library. I hadn't been there much; my parents preferred I *keep-my-head-down* there too by staying to read the books, rather than risk the shame of Overdue-ness. Also, it was too quiet and the librarians too frowny. However, I'd devoured the Year Five and Six school reading books and I was hungry for more. And I now had you. So, we diluted the Judy Blumes and Michael Morpurgos and Jacqueline Wilsons with the Sweet Valley Twins and Point Horrors. Miss Cox wrinkled her nose, but what could she say? We were reading more than ever.

In fact, we started meeting at the library every Saturday. After picking a new pile of formula romances and terrors, we'd settle in the corner of the kids section and spend the morning doodling and gossiping. We'd discuss everything we didn't get a chance to mention at school every day. Or on the telephone every evening.

'What on earth do you talk about?' Mum asked. The phone company had started doing free evening and weekend calls to local numbers, so she was more surprised than bothered, but my brother would moan about needing to plug in the modem. Mum knew that you weren't Muslim, however she approved of the-new-girl-who-went-to-church-with-her-mother-every-Sunday-and-took-the-bus-to-school-all-by-herself. So, Mum told my brother to use the internet another time instead.

#

Year Five rolled into Year Six and there was brief panic over a new teacher and seat, but Mr. Bryan and you assuaged my fears. He, by the novelty of being a man and knowing how to play the guitar; you, by your words to Lula. She was as present as ever, but there was a new spring in her sprint – with the departure of Tessa from the year above for the plains of secondary school, Lula was now the fastest girl in school *and* got to sit next to you, the best at maths.

'Sophie,' Lula said to you one playtime, 'let's be best friends.'

I was standing right next to you. But Lula made me feel like a ghost and I wanted to dissolve into the concrete. We'd never said it... But I thought that...

'Thanks!' you said and the temperature dropped. 'But I've got one.' You slipped your arm through mine.

'What, Curry Girl?!' Lula's mouth stayed open for a second, then formed a sneer. 'Her house stinks of curry, you know!'

You tightened your hold, but smiled. 'Cool — I like curry!'

Lula's face fell. But she did look at me then and her eyes narrowed, before we skipped away.

#

One Monday, you weren't in school. You were rarely ill, so I started the day under a cloud. I asked, 'Sir, where's Sophie?'

Mr. Bryan was going around the room checking our sums and mumbled, 'Oh, sudden family emergency. I'm sure it's nothing to worry about.'

Emergency? I got the rest of my sums wrong.

Later, even though there was ice-cream sandwich for pudding, I gave mine to Fairooz.

'Thanks, Najma! Where's Sophie? She's always in! I wonder what's up?' Fairooz' eyes looked even bigger than usual and she spoke with her mouth full.

I shrugged, feeling as empty as Fairooz's bowl.

'*I* know why Sophie's not in.' Lula's voice lobbed in from the other end of our dinner table.

I stiffened, but didn't look.

'We go to the same church. Yesterday, her dad came.' She paused.

I whipped my head around.

Lula smirked. 'He asked the minister if they could talk. Sophie's mum wasn't sure, but Sophie looked like she was gonna vomit.'

I got up, dumped my dirty plate on the trolley and flew towards the playground. Lula's voice echoed through the canteen and I felt it chasing me, just as I could feel her eyes boring into my back.

I called your number as soon as I got home. You didn't answer.

#

Lula was half right. You were back the next day, but came in at the last bell and sat without a word. I couldn't see your face, but felt some relief when you brushed off Lula. We had a maths test, so no one else bothered you, and Mr. Bryan even told Lula off for talking.

At playtime, I pulled towards you as soon as I could, then hung there like elastic. *What if you were avoiding me?* But you caught my eye and arm and we rushed over to the arches.

It was your dad. He'd wanted to talk to your mum, but she'd kept fobbing him off. So, he came to church. You felt sick all afternoon, and the next day. Who the hell did he think he was?

Your fists shook and I grabbed them. 'What does he want?'

'Us,' you spat. 'And Mum's actually considering it.' Your nostrils flared.

I swallowed. 'It might be a good thing.'

'That's what the minister said. That dad's repented, has a good life now and wants to share it. That mum's struggled alone for too long and we should forgive—' you stopped, your eyes were like blazing comets.

I squeezed your hands. 'Can you?'

'Dunno.' You lifted your eyes. 'He doesn't live in London, though. He's in Glasgow. He wants us to move up there.'

Glasgow? It might as well be another planet. It sounded as empty and heavy as the end-of-break bell that suddenly tolled, loud and low.

#

The winter term stretched like a rubber band, loosening and tightening with every development in your parents' talks. One Saturday, while our classmates wondered what Christmas presents they wanted and to which secondary schools to apply, we were at our usual table in the library, pouring over a title from the 'New books' display.

Dwarves, Giants, Supernovae, Nebulae. It was all about stars, full of facts and in glorious colour. I gorged on the bright hues and you whistled at the numbers.

As ever, I was drawn to the nebulae. It was five years since they'd launched Hubble, and the book featured its best photos. The Eagle, Horsehead, Crab, Butterfly, Cat's Eye. They were all in there, as well as Orion. We lingered over a picture of the Eagle Nebula's 'Pillars of Creation'. '...never-before-seen details of three giant columns of cold gas bathed in the scorching ultraviolet light from a cluster of young, massive stars,' I read aloud. They were like inky elephant trunks, raised and haloed against an emerald ocean. 'Look at that,' I said. 'It's as pretty as Orion.'

'Seven thousand light years away,' you added. 'Why d'you like these so much?' you asked suddenly. 'It's just distant dust and gas.'

I raised my eyebrows. 'Well, it's not like I wanna be a scientist, like you. I just think they look cool.'

'Engineer. Those colours are fake, anyway. They use filters, to let in certain wavelengths of light. To see what elements and stuff are there.'

'I dunno about all that.' I frowned. 'I just like them. And I thought you did too.' I looked at my hands.

You sighed. 'I do. I just don't want you thinking they really look like that.' You closed the book and took a piece of paper from your pocket. 'Anyway, here, it's my new address. Mum's decided, Najma. We're moving to Scotland.'

I stared. 'When?' I managed.

'Next week.'

'Before Christmas? It's only in two weeks!'

'Dad can't take any more time off work to keep coming back and forth. Plus mum found a new job there in another branch, she has to start straightaway.'

I'd known it was coming, as inevitable as a supernova. But knowing couldn't help.

You leaned in. 'You'll write, won't you? I'll write and send you the new number.'

'Of course. It's just so far away.' My voice was as hollow as the column of space I already saw expanding between us. We were going on eleven years old, supposed to finish primary school, and supposed to begin big school together.

'Actually, is it?' You opened the book again and flipped through it. 'There!'

I looked. 'Sirius?'

'The brightest star in our sky, right? We're still under the same sky. If you look at it every night, or whenever you feel lonely, then you'll know I'm looking at it too. With you.'

#

I wish I could say that you stayed. Or that you went and then came back, bewailing the weather. But you didn't. As numb as the December rains, I dragged myself through the rest of that term, waiting for your letter. Finally, it was the last day before the Christmas holidays. Everyone else was as fluttery as the fairy lights. There were cards and crackers and tinsel and treats, Mr. Bryan even got out his guitar. But, to me, it was like the moment after you read the lame joke from the cracker, which falls empty.

#

Christmas came and went, and still no letter. Mum reckoned you were busy and said the post was unreliable this time of year, but as the temperature plummeted, so did my hopes. I was sure you'd write, about Glasgow and your new life and friends. But you didn't.

I still had your note with the address and I hadn't forgotten about Sirius. But as the days wore on, I felt stupid looking for it when you hadn't written. So, I stood in the dark and looked out of my bedroom window one more night that winter. I was facing south west and I should have had a clear view, but I wasn't sure, and Orion's Belt wasn't visible to point the way. Your note was in my hand and for a second I considered writing to you first, but—

—FIZZ... WHISTLE... BANGBANGBANG!

I stared in horror as the sky caught on neon fire. How could I forget New Year's Eve? God knows what everyone was celebrating anyway. I don't know how long I stood there wiping my eyes and clutching your note before I decided.

I tore up the paper and threw it in the bin.

#

Year Six became Year Seven. The rest of secondary school became sixth form, then uni. Then came work, marriage and a baby... And there was me, still in south London, *keeping-my-head-down*, as life became a steady stream of work projects and child's play.

There wasn't another best friend. Different friends for my different selves were fine with me. And there were always the hubby and the baby, of course.

One day after work, after picking up Nafisa from nursery, playing with her, feeding her and putting her to bed, I realised it was an anniversary.

Hubble's twenty-fifth.

Incredible images on the news. Icons revisited, ones I used to love, including a new shot of the last one I looked at properly.

'...photographed in near-infrared, as well as visible light,' I read, 'transforming the pillars into wispy silhouettes seen against a background of myriad stars... Newborn stars can be seen hidden away inside... Transitory... We have caught these pillars at a very unique and short-lived moment in their evolution...'

I was on the NASA website and gazed at the once solid looking columns. Now more translucent, but even more beautiful to me, despite knowing that the ghostly bluish haze around them was in fact matter heating up before being evaporated away into space.

I shuddered. I remembered a girl, from twenty years ago, who'd seen a similar picture, alongside another girl.

The front door opened and I heard my husband Sohail in the hallway, shedding his shoes and jacket.

'Hi love!' He breezed into the kitchen, hair a windswept mop of curls and eyes as bright as his yellow jumper. I was sitting at the breakfast bar in front of my laptop and he leaned down to give me a kiss. 'You okay?' he said, noticing my full, stone-cold coffee cup.

"Course.' I tore my eyes away and smiled up into his. 'Sorry, was miles away.'

'So I see.' Sol grinned, then slid onto the next stool, folding his long limbs around him. He cocked his head at the laptop. 'Star-gazing?'

'Actually, I was thinking of someone I used to know. Back in primary school.'

'What happened to her?'

'I don't know. She knew more about this stuff, was really good at maths, was going to be an engineer. She was my best friend.' I paused. 'But I never told her that. Then she left.'

I saw the questions shooting across my husband's face and his mouth parted as if he would speak. But he kissed my temple and drew his arm around me instead.

I closed my eyes, grateful for the tall, warm man holding me.

You would have liked him too.

#

That night, I kept thinking of stars and little brown girls with blue hair bobbles until it was pointless staying in bed. Thankfully, Nafisa slept through the night now and Sol slept like a log, so I didn't worry about light falling across their beds as I drew the curtain aside.

I just wanted to see the stars.

One would do. It didn't even have to twinkle. It could be cold and chalky, like a full stop on a blackboard.

Not a distant bulb, or an airplane, or a bug. An actual star. Then I could stop shivering at my window and go back to bed. Even though I couldn't sleep and I'd be up again in a few hours.

Just one star. Burning away, light years from here, already dying, maybe already dead.

At least I'd know it was real.

But there was too much cloud and glare from the lampposts and houses and cranes. Why were they allowed to keep building in every patch of skyline in London? Who the hell could afford those flats anyway, and why would you want a view of yet another block of flats?

Sol's arm snaked around my waist and made me jump.

'Sorry,' he whispered, voice thick with sleep. 'Star-gazing again?'

I smiled; nothing got past him. 'I was thinking about Sophie. We were supposed to stay in touch, but we never did. We were only friends for a year, but we were really close. I know, it's silly—'

'—No, it's not. And that's a long time when you're young.' He nodded at the cot, then placed his chin on my shoulder. 'Why don't you try to find her?'

I raised my eyebrows and turned around, facing him in the fake star-light. Even half asleep, he was as hopeful and fearless as a sunrise, the brightest star in my sky. I smiled and reached up for a proper hug. 'Thank you.'

He squeezed back. 'You're welcome. Now young lady, *bed*. Those stars will still be there tomorrow.'

#

A few hours later, a breezy Saturday morning, I was out with Nafisa, who was snoozing in the buggy. We were on our way back from the shops, but all morning Sol's words were like drops of ink spreading across the pages of my mind.

Should I try to find you? What if you didn't want to be found?

I put on the brakes, leaning my forearms on the handlebar. I realised I was on a different route home, one that led me past somewhere I hadn't been in years. My heart began to thump as I looked up at the tall Victorian stone-embellished building with its sand coloured shell and treasure trove of books inside. It was more grubby and weather-worn now, but it was still there, our old hangout and haven.

I didn't go in. The breeze picked up and Nafisa stirred in protest at the lack of motion, so I released the brakes and moved on. But I kept turning over my memories all the way home.

That evening, I watched the little one practise her toddle in front of the TV while we watched CBeebies. As Nafisa babbled and waved her Igglepiggle plushie at his on-screen counterpart, I marvelled at how quickly she'd grown. Sol was out playing football with his friends, so it was just us. Perhaps one Saturday I could go to the library again, with her. Perhaps one day she'd read the same books. And perhaps one day she'd share them with someone else.

'Wah!' Nafisa waddled over and tried to eat my legs. I realised that TV Igglepiggle was asleep in his boat and drifting off under the stars again, so I gathered up my own little Igglepiggle in my arms, and headed upstairs to get her ready for bed.

Later, long past everyone's bedtimes, I couldn't sleep again. Sol, tired after footie and the post-match feast, didn't stir as I pulled on my dressing gown and headed downstairs. I got some paper and sat at the breakfast bar. Then I picked up a pen.

I don't know if I'll find you. But if I do, I'll be sure this time. I'll be sure to tell you what that year meant to me. As sure as the Orion and Eagle nebulae are awesome. As sure as the Sweet Valley Twins and Point Horrors are the greatest tweenage books ever written. As sure as Sohail and Nafisa are the brightest star and most precious gem in my world.

And maybe I'll start by writing you a letter. Well, Sophie, it has been twenty years, so I thought I'd jog your memory...

Love,

Najma

About the Authors

Farah Ahamed is a short fiction writer. Her stories have been published in *The Massachusetts Review, Thresholds, Kwani?, The Missing Slate* and *Out of Print* among others. She has been nominated for The Caine and The Pushcart prizes, highly commended in the 2016 London Short Story Prize and shortlisted for the SI Leeds Literary Prize, DNA/Out of Print Award, Sunderland Waterstones Award, Gerald Kraak Award and Strands International Short Story.

Jamilah Ahmed was born in Dubai and is half Arab, half Irish. She has lived in London since graduating from University. She has a PhD from Goldsmiths, where her work examined the female embodied self. Jamilah works in publishing, previously as a Commissioning Editor in the social sciences and more recently as a freelance editor and agent. Her writing career began with an OU online course. Following a *GoldDust* mentorship, her work has been longlisted by *Mslexia* & *WriteIdea*, and shortlisted for the Si Leeds Literary Prize 2016.

Meera Betab is a welfare rights lawyer and writer from West London. Her short stories and novel in progress are influenced by her Indian Panjabi heritage and span diverse historical and geographical settings. She was a winner of the City University's inaugural Novel Studio Competition 2014 in conjunction with the Christine Green Author's Agency. A beneficiary of author mentoring under the WoMentoring Project, her novel in progress is a mystery set in Mughal India which explores inter-faith themes.

Lynne E Blackwood is in receipt of a second Arts Council grant to complete a short story collection based on her Anglo-Indian family history. She appears in the Closure Anthology alongside well-established authors. Her character-driven crime novel set in contemporary Republic of Georgia is in submission and she is on the INSCRIBE programme, developing her poetry for a chapbook. Apart from writing and editing, Lynne is learning to play the piano and panders to the needs of two cats and one granddaughter. Lynne recently visited Andalusia and explored wheelchair Flamenco for further performances of her work at festivals and events.

Namita Elizabeth Chakrabarty's novel *If Hamlet was a Girl* was longlisted for the 2016 Peggy Chapman-Andrews Award for a first novel. She is an interdisciplinary artist, working across performance and different forms of creative writing. Her critical and creative writing has been published in English, Swedish and French. She teaches writing and performance in higher education. She is on Twitter @DrNChakrabarty.

Mona Dash was born in Odisha, India, and settled in London in 2001. With a background in Engineering and Management, she works in Telecoms Solution Sales. She writes fiction and poetry and her work has been published in various journals and anthologised internationally. She has gained a Masters in Creative Writing, with distinction, from the London Metropolitan University. She is currently working towards a PhD in Area Studies. Her books include, *Dawn-drops* (Writer's Workshop, India, 2001) a collection of poetry; *Untamed Heart* (Tara India Research Press, 2016) a novel and *A certain way* (Skylark Publications UK, 2017), a collection of poetry. Website: www.monadash.net

Juhi the Fragrant is a story addict. Within her head, hidden between the pages of innumerable notebooks, and on her digital desktop—reside a vast number of characters, plots, dialogues, places and colours, that she tries to unravel and give structure to everyday. She writes, she paints, and she learns. She has had one short story published, and is attempting to finish one historical-science fiction novel, that she is afraid has taken on epic proportions.

Sadia Iqbal lives in London and is a social work manager. Her parents moved to England from Mirpur, Azad Kashmir in the 1960s and she was born in Buckinghamshire, UK. Sadia has no previous publications. Her piece relates to a childhood experience in the early 1980s.

Farhana Khalique is a teacher, voiceover and writer from south west London, where she lives with her family. She has been teaching English for over ten years, is often heard on TV as a continuity announcer for Channel 4, and her short stories have appeared in The Asian Writer and Carillon magazines. She is on Twitter @HanaKhalique.

Ashok Patel is a Lecturer in Biomedical Sciences and lives in Birmingham with his wife and son. He has written a short play, Jeevan Saathi (Life Partner), one of three short plays under the title The Cornershop, directed by Dominic Rai. After a short run at the Hawth in Crawley, The Cornershop had a national tour in 2001. He has written a radio play, Jeevan Saathi; Life Partner which was directed by Vanessa Whitburn and transmitted on BBC Radio 4.

Serena Patel juggles being a mum with writing and working part time in a law firm. She has recently joined the Golden Egg Academy working on a picture book and a novel for children. This is her first published piece.

Palo Stickland was born in the Indian Punjab and brought up in Glasgow where she worked as a teacher. From studies in creative writing at Strathclyde University and the Open University she has gained two post-graduate qualifications in creative writing. Her novel *Finding Takri* was published in August 2013. She is working on her second novel.

Farrah Yusuf was born in Pakistan and brought up in London. She writes plays, short stories and is currently working on her first novel. She took part in Kali Theatre TalkBack (2014/2015) and the Royal Court Theatre (2015) playwriting groups. Her short stories have been published in *Five Degrees: The Asian Writer Short Story Prize* (2012), SADAA *Against the Grain* (2013) and *Beyond the Border* (2014) anthologies and shortlisted for the Writeidea Short Story Prize (2014 and 2015).

Website: www.farrahyusuf.com